THE LOST
CRUSADE

THE LOST CRUSADE

HOWARD C. HUMPHREY

Pentland Press, Inc.
England • USA • Scotland

PUBLISHED BY PENTLAND PRESS, INC.
5122 Bur Oak Circle, Raleigh, North Carolina 27612
United States of America
919-782-0281

ISBN 1-57197-218-8
Library of Congress Catalog Card Number 00-130511
Copyright © 2000 Howard C. Humphrey

Printed in the United States of America

To Lynda, for her love and encouragement over our forty-five years together; and to Cathy, mother of the world's best grandchildren, Brendan and Allyson.

CHAPTER
1

Rome—Day 1

"Maybe this wasn't such a good idea, Rid," Milt Young said.

"It's only been two weeks since we sent the announcement cards, Milt, and our patrons have just started their calls. Patience my friend," Ridley Taylor replied.

Janus International had been established following a successful search for Dr. Faust's formula for making gold—a formula, which, after being found, did not work.

Taylor was a field operative for the CIA and Young the same for British Intelligence, MI6. They had worked many cases together over the years and when Milt took a disability pension after being stabbed in the Faust operation, Rid decided to retire after twenty years of being a field operative. They, together with their board of directors, started Janus to be a security consulting firm, their motto being, "We can find anything!"

The board was made up of others involved in the Faust affair: Countess Liesel Von Anton from Staufen, Germany now living in Corfu, Greece; Clark and Lyn Keene of Cape Elizabeth, Maine; and Monsignor Ricardo Corso, Curator of the Vatican Museum, serving as an advisor on antiquities.

Milt's statement about this being a mistake was prompted by the two weeks they had spent waiting for their office door to open. Both fantasized their first new client would be a very beautiful woman.

Sometimes dreams come true. At that moment the front door opened admitting a most gorgeous, raven-haired young woman. "I'd like to talk to you about a possible search," she began. "I heard of your success with the Faust list. This is a similar problem in that it's a long lost treasure of one of my ancestors."

"Sounds interesting," Ridley said.

"Right up our alley," Milt added, "please continue Ms.—"

"I'm sorry. I got ahead of myself. I'm Lady Joanna Devon from Bodmin Moor, Devonshire, England."

"A Lady Devon from Devonshire," mused Milt. "Your family must have been there a very long time."

"Yes. The ancestor in this case, the first Earl of Devonshire, James Ompree, went on the Third Crusade with King Richard. He raised a private army to support the king. He purchased three frigates and sailed from Exeter to join the Lionhearted in southern France, but that's as far as he got. King Richard required each of the earls to fund their own expedition. It seems my earl lost his funding. His men went on with other divisions of the force to the Holy Land. Ompree died in France. He sent this letter to his wife which has been in our family Bible for centuries."

"Wow, may I see that?" Rid asked with his hand outstretched. "I'll be careful."

The letter was in a picture frame under glass. It was calligraphied and difficult to make out. Milt looked over Rid's shoulder to help him with the Old English. There wasn't much about the treasure. It had been consigned to one of the earl's commanders to hide and protect. The letter was datelined in Aigues Mortes, France. The commander with the treasure was on the supply ship when it left St. Maries de la Mer. He never arrived in Aigues Mortes. The only item with special mention was a deed given to Ompree by the king before they left England.

"He was going to use it as collateral to finance the trip," Lady Joanna said. Our family has always thought that we probably own a great portion of Devonshire and the Bodmin Moor National Park. I don't care about the park but I would like to get our castle back in the family. I'm not certain when or how it got out of the family. Probably to pay off debts created by the crusade. The present owner is Sir Dean Floyd."

"He's the head of the World Peace Foundation," Milt commented, "the one proposing to the United Nations and the major world powers that they privatize their peacekeeping armies and let the foundation run them under contract. To assure world peace, they say, and to fix lower military budgets."

"That's him," Joanna replied. "I will say there are a lot of comings and goings at the castle. He must have over one hundred employees and they operate around the clock. The other villagers of Bodmin Moor and I wonder what is going on up there. That's why I'd like to find that deed, so we can get our community back to the quiet village it's always been."

"You have come to the right place, Lady Joanna," Rid began his sales pitch. "Actually, there's quite a lot to go on. We've got the two towns in France, the names of his ships, and the date, A.D. 1188. You are our first customer, so we'll take the case for actual expenses only, plus twenty percent of any treasure found other than the deed. Okay?" Milt asked.

"Oh, yes. You're hired."

CHAPTER
2

At Sea—February 1188

The horses were restless as they stood on the rolling deck of the frigate *York*. The swells were over six feet and the horses sensed the uneven footing. Two of Sir Samuel Owens's yeomen were trying to keep the horses tethered to the mast. The *York* was one of three frigates purchased by Earl James Ompree of Devonshire to support Richard the Lionhearted in his holy crusade.

Pope Gregory VIII proclaimed the Third Crusade on 29 October 1187. The Second Crusade had failed leaving Saladin controlling everything from the Libyan Desert to the Tigris Valley. Jerusalem surrendered to Saladin on 2 October, prompting the pope's call. Enthusiasm for this crusade was widespread among Western Europe's nobility. In addition to Richard I of England, Philip II of France and Frederick I, the Holy Roman Emperor, agreed to raise armies to oust the Muslim ruler from Palestine. Each of the monarchs, in turn, solicited their knights and nobility to join them. The knights would train the collective army. The nobles were to provide the men, ships, supplies, and financing. Earl Ompree of Devonshire had raised an army of two hundred men, twenty horses, three ships, supplies, and a waterproof iron chest full of his family's fortune.

Just before leaving the port at Exeter in February, King Richard called Ompree to his court at Tintagel.

"Thank you, James, for your support in this most holy of undertakings," the king began. "You have been quick to raise your army and I know you have committed your family's fortune. I want to do something in return. I have, this day, decreed that all lands lying between your castle at Bodmin Moor and Launceston be in your family forever."

"Thank you, Your Majesty, I will add this to my committed support of this crusade. It is yours to recall if we find ourselves in need of funds during the expedition," Ompree replied.

"With God on our side, I am certain we will have plenty to rescue the Holy Land. Now, tell me about your army."

"We have two hundred men at arms, twenty on horseback, and three excellent commanders from Devonshire, sir!"

"Who are these leaders?" the Lionhearted asked.

"Sir Donald George of Dartmoor will command the ship, *Northwind,* named for his estate. Sir Seaborn Hillis of Exeter is leading the men on the *Southern Star,* and Samuel Owens from the midlands, who has christened our supply ship the *York* for his hometown."

"Good men all. Your force will be an important part of our holy crusade. Sail when you are ready. We will all rendezvous in the spring at Marseilles. I have assigned the port of Aigues Mortes for you to wait out the winter months. It's up the Rhone delta in the Camargue. You may be able to add to your horses as there are wild horses throughout that region."

"Thank you, my king. We will be ready to sail within thirty days."

"One more thing. I want to assign an experienced knight to train your men in battle. He should travel with you and carry the same rank as your commanders. He is Wallace Becker of Saxon, a most ferocious fighter and one of my most trusted knights."

"I have heard of his exploits, Your Majesty. We welcome him and look forward to his advice."

"I will see you in Marseilles in the spring, James. I know you still have much to do."

"By your leave, my lord."

* * * * *

Sir Samuel Owens had come on deck to help his two yeomen calm the horses. He knew they were approaching the Pillars of Hercules that separated the open sea from the calmer waters of the Mediterranean. The *York* was third in line in the earl's small armada. The *Northwind* and the *Southern Star* had already passed through the strait and now it was the *York*'s turn to challenge the winds and crosscurrents.

"These horses are jumping too much, sire," called one of the yeomen.

"We will have to hobble them," Sir Samuel replied.

They were working on their fifth mount, trying to tie his back legs together when the ship passed the Pillars and the seas became calmer.

"We made it," yelled the helmsman.

"Yes," responded Owens, "we have passed our first tribulation. But I suspect there will be more." How right he was!

CHAPTER
3

South of France—March 1188

Earl James Ompree's three ships were anchored in the harbor at St. Maries de la Mer. The village sat at the very bottom of the Rhone River delta and at the edge of the Camargue, a low-lying wasteland of swamp and saw grass. St. Maries was a gypsy stronghold run by its own king of the gypsies, Oleg Havrilka. Ompree and his commanders and knights were in the village negotiating with Havrilka on the toll to be levied for them to take their ships up the river to Aigues Mortes.

"I am a poor man," Havrilka said, "a simple peasant trying to make a life in this swamp. By your ships and your clothes I can tell you are men of means. Ten gold coins and I will personally assure your safe passage to Aigues. Ten more and I can assure you a safe stay for as long as you are there. And when you leave, I will give you free passage back to the sea."

"Too much," replied Ompree. "We are on a mission to drive the Muslims out of the Holy Land. We need all our gold to finance this crusade."

"I take no sides in these matters. Nor do I care who rules a land far away. We gypsies are forever free to roam and call wherever we are home. Twenty gold pieces and you'll be safe."

"Perhaps a visit to our ships will soften your stance, Oleg," insisted the knight warrior, Wallace of Saxon.

"Yes," added Sir Donald George.

"We have two hundred men at arms, you bandit," volunteered Sir Seaborn Hillis.

Sir Samuel Owens chipped in with, "And supplies and arms to be self-sufficient. We don't need your protection, you cur!"

"Do not underestimate the extent of our control of this area," Havrilka said, "but I am a reasonable man. Ten pieces of gold for both passage and protection throughout your stay."

"I will pay you five," Ompree offered.

"Eight," said the king.

"Six," countered the earl.

"You drive a hard bargain, sir. I can take no less than seven. I would be exiled from the gypsies if I got less."

"Done."

Sir Owens asked, "Do you have a map showing the way to Aigues Mortes?"

"Ha, ha!" the gypsy replied. "There are hundreds of ways to Aigues and they all crisscross. This river delta stretches throughout the Camargue. But as long as you are going upriver, you should reach Aigues Mortes. Of course, I could provide guides for a fee."

"We are quite capable of navigating our ships upriver," said the earl. "We will leave you here to steal from the next adventurers who stumble on this place."

Before returning to their ships, Ompree suggested that they stay in the wider channels while heading upriver. If anyone got lost they were to send word by messenger to Aigues, marking the trail as they traveled on foot. Ompree held Owens back, as the others returned to their ships.

"Samuel, I am worried about this gypsy. I am sure his followers are cutthroats and highwaymen who will come after the treasure. I want you to pick a place to bury it on the way to Aigues. We will transfer the men you are carrying to the other ships. Keep only six of your most trusted squires to help you navigate the river and to bury the chest, then draw a map for my eyes only."

"Yes, Sir James. You can count on me."

CHAPTER
4

Sir James was growing more anxious by the hour. The *Northwind* and *Southern Star* had arrived in Aigues Mortes the day before. Samuel Owens, on the *York*, was to have hidden their treasure trove somewhere in the river delta and then followed the earl to Aigues. Sir James called his commanders together.

"We must search for the *York*," he began, "they should have arrived last evening. Seaborn, you take your men on the *Southern Star* and retrace our route to St. Maries de la Mer. Look in the side estuaries. Donald and Sir Wallace, with your men, make your way by foot. I'll ride with Seaborn. When we meet at the bottom we will capture the town and that so-called gypsy king. I suspect he is involved in this. Now, let us go and find the *York*!"

Making their way by ship was easy now that they had mapped the course of the river's main channels. No sign of the *York* was found. They stopped around the bend from the town of St. Maries to wait for the land force.

The land group followed a narrow path, big enough for an oxcart, the only path through the Camargue. After a two-hour march, one of the men spotted a mast sticking up above the saw grass. They hacked and waded their way to the *York*, which was run aground on a sandbar. Sir Donald had an ominous feeling. A quick search revealed there was no one on board. The treasure chest, horses, and most of the supplies were gone.

"Have the men spread out to search the area. Perhaps we can find something that will tell us what happened," Knight Wallace of Saxon offered.

"Yes. From the position of the ship, I would say it drifted downriver before landing on the bar, so we should concentrate our search upriver," Sir Donald replied.

After two hours of searching, they did find horse prints in the mud. They were headed south toward St. Maries. Sirs Donald and Wallace decided to refloat the *York* and speed downriver to join Ompree. Before departing they built a marker to show where they found the ship.

They met the earl where he was at anchor in the main channel around the bend from the gypsy stronghold. They formed a battle plan for Sir Wallace to take half the men and come in by road. Sir Donald was to command the *York* and *Sir Seaborn* the *Southern Star* as they made a fast entry into the port. The gypsies were alerted when their newly found horses began to whinny.

The battle raged on between the wooden clubs, spears, and arrows of the gypsies and the iron-tipped lances and arrows of the crusaders. In the end it was the iron that made the difference. After seeing over half of his band of brigands killed, the gypsy king surrendered.

"You, Havrilka, are a scoundrel," Earl Ompree shouted. "We paid you for safe passage and your own men have stormed one of our ships and stolen our stores."

"They acted on their own," Havrilka answered. "I knew nothing of this until I saw them bringing your horses into town. I was, of course, going to return them."

"What about my men on the *York*?"

"A most unfortunate thing. My leader says your men attacked them first. They had to defend themselves. Our band had yours outnumbered threefold and, in the skirmish, your men were all killed. They were buried in the swamp."

"I will try you for their murder and see you come under the executioner's ax," Ompree said. "Sir Wallace, take as many men as you need to thoroughly search this village and gather everything that is ours. Donald, we will load it back on the *York*."

"Yes, sir!" they said in unison.

"Be particularly attentive to finding a large iron chest. It has our crusade's fund inside."

"I know nothing of a chest," Oleg pronounced. "It is not here."

"Do you mind if I don't believe you," retorted Sir James.

The search did uncover nearly all the stores, food, and weapons that were on the *York*. The chest, however, was not found.

"Do you think that Samuel hid the chest before he was attacked?" *Sir Seaborn* asked.

"It is possible, but he was to have made a map," said the earl.

"Maybe the attack came too soon, before he had a chance to draw the map," said Sir Donald.

"It is possible. Or he could have destroyed it when the attack began," the earl said, hopefully. "We must organize a search from where you found the *York*, up the river and all of the side channels. Look for signs of recent digging or footprints."

"You know, Samuel could have heaved it overboard when the gypsies attacked," mused Hillis.

"Right, Seaborn. You take Sir Wallace back to where he found the *York* and begin a water search from there, then all return to Aigues Mortes this evening. We can continue the search tomorrow."

After two long weeks of searching, it became apparent the chest would not be found. Several interrogations of the gypsies convinced the earl that they did not have the chest. It was time to tell King Richard of their disaster. Earl Ompree, Sir Wallace, and ten men at arms made their way on horseback to Marseilles, where the king was wintering. The plan was for him to leave the first of April. All of his army and that of the French king, Philip II, were to meet in Marseilles. From there, they would sail as an armada to Ostia, the port of Rome, to join forces with those of the Roman emperor, Frederick I. From there they would sail first to Turkey and then on to the Holy Land.

The earl became despondent as they got closer to Marseilles. He had failed his king and his God. He knew he would rot in Hades for his failure.

"What can I say, Your Majesty? I have failed you. I should forfeit my title and my life."

"That won't be necessary," the king said. "Your men and ships can join Sir Thomas Byerly of Oxford's command. I order you to return to England to make your claim on the lands I decreed. You look too ill to go on with us."

That proved a valid prediction. The earl returned to Aigues Mortes where he contracted pneumonia and died a few weeks later. As he lay in his bed waiting for death to arrive, he wrote a letter to his wife, Helen Ompree. It said:

My Darling Helen,

My life is coming to an end and my thoughts are of you and the love we shared. I failed miserably my king and his holy crusade. We lost the treasure that was to be our support. Gypsies killed Samuel Owens, along with fourteen other good men, six of them protecting our stores on the ship and eight more during the recovery of the supplies. My men and ships are to join with Sir Thomas of Oxford to go on with the crusade. King Richard has ordered me home on a supply ship scheduled to leave Marseilles on 2 April. 1 fear I will not last that long, but will see that this letter is delivered to you.

I owe the ship merchants a large sum for our vessels. I pledged Bodmin Castle as collateral. Should they attempt to foreclose, tell them King Richard decreed a grant to me of all the lands from Bodmin Moor to Launceton, so they will be compensated once the grant is in place. Unfortunately, the grant proclamation bearing the king's royal seal was lost with the other treasure. I did not feel I warranted another copy, so I did not tell the king.

Worse than death is leaving you with this problem.

With all my love,
Your loving husband, James.

CHAPTER

5

"This is really interesting," Ridley Taylor said as he finished the earl's letter. "Do you know what happened to them at Bodmin Moor, Lady Joanna?"

"Please call me Jo. That's the name I like to use."

"Okay," Milt Young agreed, "do you know anything about Lady Helen?"

"Yes, as the earl had feared, the ship merchants did take the castle in payment for the ships. The family also had a manor house that had been used as a wayside inn at the edge of Bodmin Town. Lady Helen moved in there and it has been our family home ever since. The lady and her serfs were hired to continue to work the land so she did have an income."

"Did she try to have the king's decree for more land honored?" asked Rid.

"I'm not certain. She felt it was her husband's dying wish not to perfect the claim. I do know a much later ancestor made a try around 1600. From his note in the family Bible, the government turned him down saying he would need the original document. We have not tried it since, but with my concern about what is going on at the castle, I felt now is the time. And, as I said, I heard about your success with Faust's five hundred-year-old list."

"It is well worth trying to find the trunk, although it's likely that someone through the centuries has already plundered the treasure," Milt tried to check Jo's enthusiasm.

"Or it still could be buried in the Camargue. If it was waterproof and is buried in mud, it may still be intact," Ridley countered. "I suggest we go see Monsignor Corso to find out what the Vatican records have about the crusades."

"A great idea, Rid. I'll call his office and make an appointment for tomorrow. I'll also call the countess and the Keenes to ask them to make suggestions on what we should do."

Milt went in the other office to make his calls. Rid got on his computer and printed everything his online encyclopedia had on the crusades. He paraphrased it to Jo.

"The crusades began formally on Tuesday, 27 November 1095, in a field just outside the walls of the French city of Clermont-Ferrand. On that day Pope Urban II preached a sermon to crowds of laypeople and clergy attending a church council at Clermont. In his sermon the pope outlined a plan for a crusade. He also outlined a basic strategy: Individual groups of crusaders would begin their journey in August 1096. Each group was to be self-financing and responsible to its own leader.

"The First Crusade went well with major victories at Nicaea and Antioch. They finally took Jerusalem by storm on 15 July 1099. They massacred every resident. In the crusader's view, the city was purified in the blood of the defeated infidels.

"That act prompted the unification of Muslim forces in the Middle East. Under Zangi, the Muslims began to retake territories they had lost. The papacy's response was to proclaim the Second Crusade late in 1145. It failed in its mission as its German army was attacked in ambush at Anatolia. Few survived. The French had some success, but were then defeated at Damascus in July 1148. Following that and Saladin's succession to power, the Third Crusade was called by Pope Gregory VIII. We know what happened there. It says here the crusading forces reached Palestine and held the port city of Haifa. They never retook Jerusalem and finally many of the crusaders simply went home. King Richard returned to England to deal with his troublesome brother, John.

"There were several more crusades up until 1270, but none of them had the success of the first or third. You might call the third 'The Last Crusade.' In honor of your ancestor, I think I will name it 'The Lost Crusade.'"

"Thank You, Rid," Jo said with a smile. "May I call you Rid?"

"Only if you will have dinner with me tonight."

"What about Milt?"

"He has a steady girlfriend at the British Embassy. We could invite them but I would rather have you to myself."

"Do I hear you two plotting against me?" Milt said as he reentered the room.

"No plot, Milt. I was just inviting Jo to dinner. I assume you have plans with Marlene."

"As a matter of fact, I do. There is a reception at our embassy for the Premier of Nepal and I have been invited. We are on with Monsignor Corso at ten tomorrow."

"All right, let's plan to meet here at nine and we'll go together to the museum," Rid replied.

"The other members of our board are excited about the project and will fax their suggestions overnight, so leave the fax turned on. Good night you two."

"Good night," they both giggled.

Rid suggested, "I'll pick you up at 7:30 at your hotel."

"I'm staying at the Raphael."

"I know the place. Just off the Piazza Navonna. One of Italy's presidents lived there. We can walk to one of my favorite restaurants from there."

Dinner was set for 8:00 at La Costanza, one of Rome's finest restaurants. It was in a building that sat over the ancient Teatro Pompeii, the theatre in which Caesar was murdered and spoke the line, "Et tu, Brute!"

They were seated in the small courtyard.

"Jo, you are one knockout of a lady," Rid opened when the fusili with porcini mushroom pasta was served. "Tell me more about yourself."

"Not much to tell. My parents are both deceased. I spent most of my life in girl's schools in Switzerland. Since the death of my mother two years ago, I have been at Bodmin Moor, converting the manor house into a bed and breakfast. We no longer work the land."

"Any love interests?"

"Not currently. I guess I'm not the type that wants to be held down. What about you? You must have any number of women after you all over the globe."

"Don't I wish. Actually, as a field operative for the CIA, it's a bad idea to let anyone get close, so you form a habit of short-term relationships."

"Is that how you see me?" Jo quizzed.

"I'm not in the CIA anymore and I sure would like help in breaking my old habits. You want the job?"

"I might!" Jo replied as their main course of ossobuco was served,

After dinner, they walked back through the Piazza Navonna like two schoolchildren hand in hand. At the door of the Raphael, Rid kissed her lightly on the lips. He then walked jauntily to his car whistling "What a Wonderful World."

CHAPTER
6

Rome—Day 2

Milt was already at his desk when Rid arrived at 8:45 the next morning.

"So did you take good care of our client last night, Rid?"

"Very good care. We had dinner at Costanza and an evening stroll through Piazza Navonna. She is staying at the Raphael."

"Was her room nice?" Milt asked innocently.

"I'm sure it was. But I didn't see it, Mr. Nosy."

They studied the earl's letter again and began to make a list of things to do. They thought Monsignor Corso would be helpful both for his knowledge of history and for whatever the Vatican library might have on Pope Gregory VIII's records. A trip to the Camargue to see the area would at least define the magnitude of the problem and help them visualize a search pattern for the chest.

"I think I'll call Bryan Roberts, my old boss at the CIA," Rid said. "Maybe I can have him order some satellite pictures when one of our 'spies in the sky' flies over the Camargue."

"Yes," added Milt, "have them send us the information from the satellite used to track submarines."

"How do you know about that? It's classified."

"MI6 was in the business of gathering information, remember."

"Do I hear my newfound heroes quibbling?" Lady Joanna said as she entered the office.

"No quibble," Rid replied. "I was just accusing Milt of stealing U.S. Government secrets."

"I am a trained spy, you know," Milt chortled. "How was your evening with my accuser?" Milt asked to double-check Rid's story.

"He was a perfect gentleman, dammit," Jo joked.

They all laughed. Then Milt and Rid explained the things they were planning to do.

"That sounds good. I think you also should come to Bodmin Moor to look at my family records and to see Bodmin Castle. Maybe you can get an idea of what Sir Dean is doing up there."

"Good idea. We'll add that to our list," Milt said. "I'd like to visit the Home Secretary's Office in London to research the process for filing a king's decree. I wonder if it's ever been done."

"It is now 9:30. We better be on our way to see our friend and advisor Monsignor Corso," Ridley said as they all got up to leave.

CHAPTER
7

Rome—Day 2

Their taxi arrived at the employee's entrance to the Vatican Museum at ten minutes to ten. The line at the visitor entrance was four abreast and wound around the Vatican City walls for three hundred yards.

"If you plan to visit the museum, Jo, either ask the monsignor for a VIP pass or come at 8:15 to get in line. They open at 8:45 and you would be in the first group admitted," Rid suggested.

"Oh, I've seen it. And I stood in a line much like this one. The Sistine Chapel made it all worthwhile."

"You're going to like Ricardo, that is, Monsignor Corso," Milt said. "He is one of the world's foremost experts on antiquities. We are very fortunate to have him as an advisor to Janus."

"In fact, he gave us our company's name," added Rid.

"How's that?" she asked.

"After we found the Faust notes of his trying to make gold from base metal, we came here to test it on an old apparatus that was made by Leonardo DaVinci while he was here working for the pope. The monsignor used an old Roman coin crucible to pour in our molten metal. Unfortunately the gold turned out to be worthless, but the coin became our corporate logo. It had the bust of Janus on it."

"Is he the one with two heads?" Jo interrupted Rid.

"Two faces actually on one head, one looking forward and one looking back. He was the keeper of the gate, of all comings and goings, the future as well as the past. The month of January is named for him. We think it symbolizes everything we're trying to do," Ridley finished.

"That's good," she said as they entered the building.

As Rid and Milt had been there a number of times discussing the set up for Janus, the guard recognized them immediately.

"The monsignor is expecting you. You know the way, so go right on up."

They took the elevator to the fifth floor. When they got off they were in a very large room that served as a workshop for the staff working on new additions to the museum and making repairs or restorations. Articles for the museum came in a steady flow from all over the globe. At the far end of the room was a glassed-in office with a window looking out over the Vatican gardens.

As they approached the office, a tall, handsome man with white hair and well-trimmed beard came out from behind the desk and said, "You must be Lady Joanna. Milt told me about your letter from an ancestor in the crusades. I am very excited to see it."

"Please call me Jo. I don't use the title."

"All right, Jo, and you can be like my two friends here and call me Ricardo."

As they sat down in the office, Milt removed the framed letter from his leather portfolio. "Here it is, Ricardo. Do you think it is genuine?"

"We can soon tell that. I will have it carbon dated if you leave it with me."

"That would be wonderful," Jo agreed.

"I've been thinking about this problem since you called yesterday. There are several places here we can look. Our library will have all of Pope Gregory VIII's history as recorded by his scribes. And we have a large collection from the crusades with names of people and ships. We even have some of the old ships' logs for the time before they left Rome. The pope renamed the ships for saints and gave them new logs for the crusade."

"Wouldn't that be a stroke of good fortune if you had the log of the *York*, *Northwind*, and *Southern Star*," Milt said enthusiastically.

"I'll have our senior librarian search for them. Give me one day and I'll see what I can find. Can you come again tomorrow at the same time?"

"We'll be here!" all threereplied.

"Until tomorrow then," the priest said. "What a delightful problem."

CHAPTER
8

Rome—Day 3

Ridley Taylor, Milt Young, and Lady Jo Devon met at nine the next morning at the Janus International office.

"Any suggestions from our board members, Milt?" asked Rid.

"The Keenes like what we've planned. They said we should check with the harbormasters at both Aigues Mortes and St. Maries de la Mer. Perhaps they have a report of the trunk being found."

"Good idea," said Jo. "What about the countess?"

"She and her three dowager tenants must have come up with this one during the vodka portion of their afternoon 'tea.' They say rent some of those metal detectors like you see on the beach and comb the Camargue," Milt finished his report.

"That's not a bad idea," Rid said, "particularly if our satellite flyover pinpoints specific areas where metal is detected. I did call Bryan Roberts at the CIA yesterday evening. He said they wouldn't make a special effort or divert the spy sub chaser, but the next time its regular flight plan takes it across the Camargue, it will get extra photos for us."

"Terrific!" shrieked Jo. "I knew I had picked the right guys to get this job done."

"If only you didn't have to put up with lover boy Rid's advances," Milt responded.

"His advances to me are a lot slower than the progress you two are making on finding my ancestor's lost chest," Jo said. "He just dropped me at the hotel yesterday after lunch and said he would see me this morning."

"I wanted to be sure I was at the office to work out the deal with Bryan Roberts on the satellite," Rid replied. "Perhaps tonight I'll show you my medium fast advance."

"You saving the fast one for someone else?" she queried.

"I told you I needed help working on long-term relationships, so medium is about right for our second evening together," Rid countered.

"Enough of this verbal foreplay," said Milt. "It's time to go see the monsignor."

They arrived at the Vatican Museum at 9:45 and were sent up immediately to the curator's office. Monsignor Corso greeted them excitedly.

"Let me show you what we have found in just twenty-four hours! Please sit down," Ricardo said as he led them into his office. "First, we have found the files of Pope Gregory VIII. More importantly, his records contain a list of all the ships that left the port of Rome on the Third Crusade. It appears he had all the ships' names changed to the names of saints. Among those listed are three ships recently assigned to the command of Earl Thomas Byerly of Oxford. The *Northwind* is shown as being renamed the *Ambrose* after St. Ambrose. The *York* became the *Patrick* after the saint who rid Ireland of the snakes. The *Southern Star*, being one of the larger ships in the fleet, was named for St. Stephen."

"That's great," said Milt. "Does it say what became of the ships?"

"There is one entry that the *Patrick* was sunk off the coast of Turkey before they reached the Holy Land. We haven't found anything on the other two yet, but we are still looking."

"What else?" asked Rid.

"Our carbon dating corroborates the date on the earl's letter. It shows late twelfth century," the priest said.

"So we can treat the letter and the story of Earl Ompree as fact. But where do we start?" Milt posed the question.

"There is one more thing," Ricardo said. "Pope Gregory's records show that as the names of the ships were changed, they were given new logbooks. The old books from all the ships in the armada were sent to a monastery near Salzburg, Austria where they could be translated into Latin and German. They were to be stored in the salt mines there, where the temperature and humidity are constant. Over the centuries, the church has stored many things there."

"What's the name of the monastery?" Rid cut in.

"It is known as the Abbey at Berchtesgaden. All the best medieval scholars were sent there to research and write a true history of the world and the church for storage in the tunnels," the monsignor replied.

"Isn't Berchtesgaden where Hitler had his Eagle's Nest retreat?" Jo asked.

"The very same. The monastery sits on the next peak to the south of the Eagle's Nest," Ricardo replied. "I can set up a visit for you if you like."

"As soon as you can," Rid said. "I think this is a good place to start."

"I agree," Milt added. "If we can find the old log of the *York*, it may narrow our search considerably."

"This is exciting," Jo said, "I want to go along."

"I don't see why not," Rid said.

"I wish I were going," Monsignor Corso added, "but I will stay here and continue to review Pope Gregory's files."

Milt finished the discussion with, "We'll let you know what we find at the abbey. When can you set up our meeting with the monks?"

"I will set it up for the day after tomorrow. This will give you time to get there and them time to look for the logs," Ricardo replied.

"Thank you, Ricardo. With the snow up there, maybe I can get Joanna on the slopes tomorrow," Rid suggested.

"Remember, I went to school in Switzerland, big boy. You'll never catch me on skis," she answered.

"I hope I won't have to catch you."

"Enough of this you two. Let's go pack," Milt cut them off.

They left the Vatican very excited about what they might find at the abbey and felt they were edging closer to the long lost chest. There was also a feeling of danger that none of them could identify.

CHAPTER
9

Bodmin Castle, Devonshire, England—Day 4

While Ridley Taylor and Lady Joanna Devon were enjoying their frolic on the ski slopes just south of Salzburg at Kitzbuhl, Austria, a secret meeting of the New Millennium Foundation was about to begin. Sir Dean Floyd had assembled military leaders from around the world to hear a briefing on his plan for privatizing every nation's military forces into the foundation. He had announced a news conference to be held in three days to describe the presentation he would make to the United Nations. This meeting was far more critical and sinister. While New Millennium Foundation was the organization's actual name, Sir Dean privately referred to it as the New Millennium World Order.

His plan was quite simple. If he could convince the nations of the world to turn over their military to him by 1 January 2001, he would convert the world to a military state on that date with himself becoming the self-proclaimed dictator.

His guests began to arrive. There were top military advisors from all the members of the United Nations. Among them were: the United States Secretary of Defense and Chairman of the Joint Chiefs of Staff; England's Foreign Secretary and the head of military intelligence; the top ranking officers from the new Russia—Belarus, Ukraine, Kazakhstan, and even Chechnya; Germany, France, and the NATO pact nations sent all their highest ranking officers; plus cabinet members, generals, premiers, sheiks, and princes from other countries.

Sir Dean Floyd's goals for this meeting were to openly seek the support of the group in endorsing his U.N. proposal. Second, he wanted to surreptitiously identify individuals who he believed would join him in his new world order. After all were seated in the great hall, Sir Dean came to the podium.

"Welcome to Bodmin Castle and to the headquarters of the New Millennium Foundation. Over the next several hours, I hope to win your support for our proposal to privatize the world's military. This is a preview of what I will present to the U.N. in three weeks. It is in rough form so your comments and suggestions are welcome."

With that the room darkened, a giant screen descended from the ceiling, and a video began showing battle scenes from around the globe. The emphasis was on the loss of life and the agony of war. After about three minutes of gore, a brilliant sunrise filled the screen with the words "new millennium" across the middle. Then Sir Dean appeared on the screen and started his presentation about the value of privatizing the world's armies into a single peacekeeping force.

"The number one advantage of this proposal is to eliminate the horrors of war as you have seen here. Having one large military with no holdouts means there can be no more Iraqis, no terrorist organizations, no guerillas. There will, at long last, be peace in the Middle East, Bosnia, Northern Ireland, Sri Lanka, and other hotspots around the world.

"The other major benefit is the cost of running a large-scale military operation. We estimate we can cut each country's military budget by up to sixty percent. That will free up hundreds of billions of dollars for improved domestic production. National debts could be reduced or eliminated. Welfare and retirement systems could be enhanced.

"Very simply, we can have a millennium of world peace for less than half the expense spent on the present system which doesn't work. Now let me show you around the foundation's headquarters."

A video tour of the castle showed the large "Peace Room." It looked a lot like any war room with glass maps of the world, computer screens everywhere, and technicians working at monitors. The video ended with the picture of the sunrise. Emblazoned across the sun was the message: New Millennium = Peace and Prosperity.

As the screen went dark, Sir Dean returned to the podium. "I will answer your first question before it is asked. Any of you who support our efforts by recommending to your governments to vote for the proposal will be assured an equal rank in the new peace army. You will lead the force in your own country. And, our studies comparing military salaries to those of other industries show leadership positions need to have base pay increased by fifty percent. We also will be granting stock options for long-term capital accumulation.

"I will take other questions when we return to this hall. But first, you have seen the short version of our tour; I have asked my staff to take you in groups of twenty on a full tour. Ask all the questions you like. In addition we are now handing out a short survey that we would like to have you complete. You need not give your name, but if you are interested in joining us, there is a place at the bottom for you to identify yourself. There also is a card on which you can write anonymous questions. Now, please, enjoy your tour."

They split up by common language into groups of twenty. What started with skepticism soon became awe. Millennium had accurate inventories of people, equipment, and weapons for every nation on earth. They had also tapped into most of the military intelligence networks and even received satellite photos at the same time they were received in their home countries. Comments ranged from "Oh my God!" to "How did they get this stuff?" By the end of the tour, all were suitably impressed. They then reassembled in the great hall. Each was given a few minutes to fill out the survey, indicate their level of support, and anonymously write questions on cards to be gathered for Sir Dean's review.

Sir Dean picked up the deck of question cards and read the top one. "How did you get all of the secret information you have gathered? When you pay the highest salaries for military experts, you get the best. Plus, they can earn bonuses for projects completed on time."

He picked up the next question card. "Will you release the depth of your information at your press conference or to the United Nations? No. We will not demonstrate those capabilities to anyone who does not have top priority security clearance. By the way, we have verified all of yours."

Sir Dean read the next question. "How long do you think it will take to get all nations to buy in? We estimate that if the U.N. General Assembly accepts the proposal, we will have over two-thirds converted by 1 January 2001, hence the name 'New Millennium.'"

"Next question: What happens to holdouts? As more and more nations join, we will be so powerful that no one will defy us. We may need U.N. economic sanctions, but no military intervention is planned at this time."

"Last question: Is this a case of martial law in which you intend for your army to run the world? That wouldn't be all bad. I've always felt military leaders make the best country leaders. But to answer your question, there is nothing in the proposal about establishing a state of martial law."

"Any more questions?" Sir Dean asked.

"There probably will be a lot of questions after we go home and discuss your proposal with our various heads of state," the U.S. Secretary of Defense said. "When do you need our indication of support in order to qualify for your offer of employment with stock options?"

"I am to appear at the U.N. three weeks from yesterday. It would be helpful to know any time before then. As to my employment offer, there is no deadline. I indicated it might take two years to sign up most of the nations. Any more questions?"

There was a pause. Sir Dean Floyd closed the meeting with, "There are cocktails and a buffet in the dining room. My staff and I will be there. If you have personal questions or comments, please talk to me. Let me close by thanking you for coming. In this room are the most outstanding leaders in the world. Who better to lead our planet into the next millennium?"

CHAPTER
10

Berchtesgaden, Germany—Day 5

Ridley and Joanna were having breakfast at the Goldener Hirsch Hotel in Salzburg, when Milt Young walked in to join them.

"How were the slopes in Kitzbuhl?" he asked.

"Great!" answered Jo.

"Exhausting!" added Rid. "She didn't tell me she was a downhill racer at the World Cup five years ago. I was so tired when we got here, I just went up to my room and soaked in hot water."

"Is that the famous Ridley medium-fast move?" Milt chided.

"I'd call it dead stopped," Jo laughed. "He didn't even buy my dinner and I'm paying all expenses."

"There will be more evenings, my dear. Don't count Ridley Taylor out quite yet," he replied.

Monsignor Corso had arranged their meeting with the monks at the abbey at Berchtesgaden for 2:00 P.M. Milt had come by train to Salzburg. Rid had driven so they could bring ski equipment. It was less than an hour to Berchtesgaden, so they decided they would have an early lunch and then drive to the abbey.

"In the meantime, I'm going to call the assistant to the director at MI6," Milt said, "to see what they can tell us about Sir Dean Floyd and his New Millennium Foundation."

"Good!" said Jo. "I know something bad is going on up there."

"I'm to check late today with Bryan Roberts at the CIA about the timing of our satellite flyover of the Camargue," added Rid. "If that's going to be a few days, perhaps we should go to England next to see Bodmin Castle, and check with the government on how to perfect a royal decree."

"I think we should just plan to go to England next anyway. I'll make arrangements for you to stay with me at Ruth's Place," Jo volunteered. Ruth's Place was the name of the manor house Jo had converted into a bed and breakfast.

"Let's plan to meet at noon at St. Paul's Steuben down the street. They open early for the tourists. We can leave from there for the abbey," Milt said as he rose from the table.

"Okay," Rid said as he too rose. "Jo, let's you and I go make our phone calls. We can then meet about 10:30 and take a stroll around the city. We can go see the Hohensalzburg Castle, the cathedral, and St. Peter's Abbey."

"I'll meet you in the lobby at 10:30," Jo replied.

When Milt made his call to his old friend, Jeremy Martin at MI6, and asked about Sir Dean Floyd and Bodmin Castle, he got a lot more information than he expected.

"M was down there yesterday with military leaders from around the world to preview Floyd's proposal to the United Nations. She was very impressed with his capabilities and forthright ability to answer every question. In fact, she is meeting at this moment with the prime minister and all of our military leaders to decide whether England will support their plan."

"What is their plan?" Milt wanted to know.

"They want to privatize all the military in the world. Their slogan is 'New Millennium equals Peace and Prosperity,' meaning they can assure peace and cut defense budgets so each country can use the money for domestic programs."

"Sounds attractive, but I would be cautious about putting that much control in one person," Milt offered.

"Exactly the concern our government and that of the United States has been exploring today. We are working together to solve that concern by having the U.N. Security Council act as an oversight board to approve all senior staff changes. They would also completely review the success of the operation every three years to see if the contract should be renewed."

"That would be essential, Jeremy. What else?"

"If you would like to see their headquarters down in Devonshire, they are having a press conference the day after tomorrow. I'm certain we could arrange press credentials for you. I know M would value your opinion."

"That would be great. Could I get credentials for my partner, Ridley Taylor?"

"We would welcome his insight as well. He worked with us many times when he was a field operative for the CIA. I'll leave the credentials at the drop box at Heathrow so you can pick them up when you fly in."

"Good, Jeremy. That's really good!"

* * * * *

At the time Milt was briefing Jo and Rid over lunch in Salzburg about his call to MI6, New Millennium's Security Chief, Franz Schwartz, walked into Sir Dean's office at Bodmin Castle. Schwartz was a pure example of what the Nazis called the master race. You could see the evil in his eyes. He was tall and blond, with his hair in a crew cut. He carried a riding crop in his hand and used it frequently when eliciting information.

"Thought you would want to see this right away. It's the transcript of a telephone conversation. The call came in to Jeremy Martin about thirty minutes ago. We have identified the person calling as former MI6 operative, Milt Young," Schwartz said as he handed the paper to Floyd.

"Most interesting. Both to know we will have uninvited guests at our press briefing and the idea of involving the Security Council as our oversight. For the first, we must let Young and this Ridley Taylor attend to see if we can win them over. Assign two of your best to watch them while they are here. As to the second idea, I think agreeing to have the U.N. in control of our contract is just what we need to sell the whole plan. Think of this. If the first contract term is three years, as they suggest, and we have enough to control the military in two years, as we plan then there will be no U.N. when it is time to renew. They are just a bunch of babbling intellectuals who talk and talk but never act. We can satisfy them until we are ready."

"That's brilliant, chief, or should I call you 'Your Excellency'?" Franz quipped.

"Not quite yet, Franz, but in time. You could become the head of the world's secret service. Your first assignment is to find out more about this duo of Taylor and Young. Get their backgrounds and find out why they are interested in New Millennium."

"Yes, sir. We'll be ready for their visit to Bodmin Castle," Schwartz said as he left the room.

CHAPTER
11

Berchtesgaden, Germany—Day 5

Milt had just finished telling Rid and Jo about the MI6 offer to provide press credentials for them to the New Millennium press briefing.

"That's great, Milt," Rid said. "Once we're inside, maybe we can do a little reconnoitering on our own."

"I'd sure like to go," Jo interjected.

"No. Milt and I have a tendency to get ourselves in hot water. We're trained to get out of it too. And your beauty will give me incentive to find out all I can in a short time."

"Are you still trying, lover boy?" Milt laughed.

"At every opportunity, my man, every opportunity!" Rid countered.

"I'm beginning to think he's all talk and no action," sighed Jo.

"At the proper time, my dear. We better get going. We have to be at the abbey by two," Rid said as he pulled out Lady Jo's chair.

The drive took less than an hour, so they paused on the valley floor to look up at Hitler's retreat, the Eagle's Nest. They arrived at the abbey five minutes early. They waited by the massive wood door and then rang the bell at precisely 2:00. The door immediately swung open and a rotund monk in his cassock and slippers greeted them.

"Welcome, travelers, to our place of sanctuary. I am Brother Ignatius, a librarian responsible for our archives. We have been excited about your visit since the curator's call from the Vatican. But first, the abbot awaits us in his office."

They walked through a small vegetable garden area, into a side door of the chapel, through it to the dining room, and then into a small office. The abbot rose from his desk and came forth to welcome his guests.

"Please sit down. There are just enough seats for the five of us. I am Brother Francis. We don't get many visitors here. Usually they are scholars researching some period information for their own writings."

"We understand that you and your predecessors are responsible for much of the world's recorded history," Jo spoke first. "I am Lady Joanna Devon. I hired these two, Mr. Ridley Taylor and Mr. Milt Young, to help me find a family treasure that was lost during the Third Crusade."

"Yes. Monsignor Corso briefed us on the purpose of your visit. Brother Ignatius has good news for you. Tell them Iggy."

"We have found the ships' logbooks for your ancestor's three ships, the *Northwind*, the *York*, and the *Southern Star*. They are on the desk in front of you. But please be very careful with them. They are fragile even though they have been in our perfect storage climate in the salt mines since the twelfth century."

Each book was bound in what must have been a leather folio tied with thongs so more pages could be added. The first entry in each was dated 2 February 1188 and read, "We sailed today from Exeter, the port for Devonshire, England. We leave on a mission for God and our good King Richard. We intend to recapture the Holy Land from the infidels." From there, each log was different, containing a daily record of what happened on each ship.

Jo was fascinated reading her ancient nobleman's account of his voyage from Exeter to Aigues Mortes and of their encounter with the gypsies. The closing pages described their daily search for the lost treasure, the earl's meeting with the king, and ended with his turning over his ships and men to Sir Thomas Byerly of Oxford.

Rid was reading the log of the *York*. There were entries every day up to the loss of the treasure. The previous day it described the earl's orders to bury the treasure in the Camargue. The day of the battle with the gypsies, the only entry was, "It has dawned a day of bright sun and is warm for this time of year. We are beginning our sail up the Rhone delta to Aigues Mortes. We are taking a different route than the *Southern Star* and the *Northwind*, as I, God's servant, Samuel Owens, and six trusted seamen are to hide Sir Ompree's treasure." Another entry read, "We have been under sail and oars for over two hours and are turning from a main channel into a smaller estuary on the starboard side. We can see a group of people wading through the saw grass off to port. We should be well past them before they reach this channel, unless we run into shallow water."

"There is our first real clue to this mystery. We know the chest was on the *York* that day," Rid said. "And we know they had been traveling something over two hours, having left St. Maries de la Mer shortly after sunrise."

"I wonder how fast a ship like the *York* could travel going upstream under sail and oar?" Milt pondered.

"We have been working on that," the abbot said. "Our mathematics experts conclude that a ship like the *York* could make sixteen knots under full sail in open seas. The oars were probably used to keep the ship out of the shallows and didn't provide much propulsion. Given that, we say they were making eight or nine knots. After two hours or more they probably had gone between sixteen and thirty kilometers."

"There is one more thing we have deduced," Brother Ignatius said proudly. "The log said they saw people in the marsh. They wouldn't stop to bury the chest while there was a chance they would be seen. We understand that after the battle, the chest was not on the ship and the gypsies didn't have it. Sir Samuel must have heaved it over the side as the battle was about to begin."

"That's right," Milt added. "The *Southern Star*'s log describes how they found the *York* on a sandbar. They figured it must have floated downstream from the battleground."

"This is almost too exciting!" Jo chirped. "I'm beginning to believe we are going to find the chest."

"That's why you hired Janus, Jo," Milt said.

"We thought you might want copies of the logs. They are too fragile to photocopy, so Brother Ignatius and his group have transcribed it onto a computer file. Here they are on this floppy disk," smiled the abbot.

"I thought you worked with quill pens," Rid inquired.

"We did many years ago. But then history and progress moved much more slowly then. We have one of the largest local area networks in Europe. All of our brethren are fully trained in the systems we use."

"Thank you. And you, Brother Ignatius, have been most helpful."

"It's been fun for us," Iggy said.

"Please let us know if you find the treasure," the abbot concluded. "Goodbye, my new friends."

"Goodbye!" the three searchers said.

Once they were back in the car, they all agreed they had made huge strides toward finding the treasure. They talked about getting an old map of the Camargue to define the boundaries of where to focus their search.

"I can tell Bryan Roberts when I call him tonight, so they can take more pictures there," Rid volunteered.

"I'll get us tickets to fly into Heathrow tomorrow," Jo said.

"And I will try to find a map," Milt added.

With the excitement over finding the logbooks, they hadn't spent much time on what they might find at Bodmin Castle, but they all sensed it would be sinister.

CHAPTER
12

When they arrived at London's Heathrow Airport, Milt Young led Ridley Taylor and Lady Joanna Devon to a small, unmarked office in the administration area. Inside were several mailboxes with combination locks. "Jeremy gave me our combination. They change them with each drop." Inside the box were press credentials for both Milt and Rid, complete with press photo IDs, and an invitation to New Millennium's conference scheduled for 10:00 the next day. They rented a car and drove to Bodmin Moor in the southwest peninsula of England. The town sat at the edge of the national park by the same name. As they approached the village, they could see the castle on the hill. Storm clouds were gathering behind the castle.

"I hope that's not an omen," Jo said.

"So do we," Milt said. "So do we."

Jo showed them to their rooms at her bed and breakfast, Ruth's Place. She told them to come down to dinner at 6:30. "Let's get a little rest this afternoon."

"That's fine with me," Milt said. "I want to make a list of the things I'd like to find out about tomorrow."

Rid added, "I'd like to see a room layout for the castle."

"My family hasn't lived there for centuries, but I have early drawings of the design. I have been to parties there and could update the old setup," Jo replied.

"That's great. Let's go look at the old map."

Jo led Rid into the library and retrieved a very old Bible and a file from a locked cabinet. "You may want to read some of the old letters too. There is a little bit about the attempt to perfect the king's decree."

"Yes. Just leave me here and I will have a most interesting afternoon. What time did you say Milt and I should come to dinner? Should we dress?" Rid asked.

"Oh no. We are informal here. We have two other guests in the house who will be in the dining room. We'll talk in my sitting room after dinner. Good reading. I'll see you later," Jo said as she turned to leave the library.

Rid reached out and pulled her to him. Their embrace was like electricity, leaving them both tingling.

Jo pushed back and said, "Wow, that must be your super fast move?"

"Seize the day," Rid answered. "Carpe diem. That's my motto."

"I thought your motto was 'We can find anything.'"

"True. Unless you leave right now, I'm officially changing it to seize the day."

"Very tempting, but I also have work to catch up on since I have been gone a few days. See you at 6:30."

"I'll be there."

* * * * *

At 6:30 Rid and Milt went down the stairs together. Rid was telling him about what he had found about the castle in the old files of the Devons.

Milt said he had made up a list of things to accomplish on their visit to the press conference. They arrived in the dining room to find Jo serving another couple. There was another table set for three.

Jo called them over and introduced them to Mr. and Mrs. Harry Bentsen, travelers from Norway.

"We have been motoring around England for two weeks. We go on tomorrow down to the tip. Jeanne Shrimpton has a bed and breakfast in Penzance. We stayed there three years ago, but we like this one better," Harry said.

"Thank you, Mr. Bentsen," Jo replied. "Gentlemen, please sit over here. We're serving a lamb stew tonight. I hope you like it."

"It is very good," Mrs. Bentsen said through a mouthful of stew.

After dinner, Jo, Milt, and Rid went to Jo's sitting room.

Milt went first. "Here is a list of questions I want asked tomorrow."

42

"Others will probably ask them, but if they miss any, we can pose them ourselves. Here also is a list of things I'd like to see." Jo and Rid read the two lists. The questions were: What will be the governance structure of New Millennium? Who will be in charge within each member country? On what do you base your budget estimates? What will be the length and nature of your agreement with the U.N.? Isn't this too much power vested in one company? Where is the balance?

"All good questions, Milt. Now let's compare your list of things to see with mine from my review of the castle layout." As they discussed the two approaches to what they wanted to see, and with Jo's more current knowledge of the castle, they developed a single merged list. All wanted to see the great hall, particularly any electronic surveillance that it contained. Also, satellite antennas. How many and how big? From that they could deduce the level of their information gathering capability. Additionally, they wanted to see the "Peace Room." From viewing it, they hoped to find out if it was set up only for administration or if offensive weapons could be launched from there. They planned to look for any new structures within the castle walls, such as barracks for guards, bunkers, or warehouses for ammunition or supplies.

After considerable discussion, they all agreed the most important thing they could focus on was the communications system. From that they would know if New Millennium was capable of any covert intelligence operations. If so, they could assume that Sir Dean already knew about the United States' and the United Kingdom's counterproposal for using the U.N. Security Council as a board of directors. They also would know whether they had been exposed. If so, they felt they were entering a trap.

"Perhaps you should not go," Joanna said.

"We've been in worse," Milt said.

"Much worse!" added Rid. "Don't worry, I plan to come back to you."

They all went separately upstairs to bed. Harry Bentsen was on his cellular phone talking to Franz Schwartz who was at the castle.

"You were right, Franz. These two are planning on getting a good look at our operations tomorrow. I couldn't hear everything through the closed door, but I heard references to communications systems several times."

"Very good, Harry. You and Mina go on to Penzance tomorrow. Then come back here on Saturday."

CHAPTER
13

Bodmin Moor—Day 7

Mr. and Mrs. Bentsen were finishing their breakfast, when Ridley entered the room. "Nice day, ja?" Harry Bentsen said.

"Yes, sunny and warm for this time of year," Rid added. "You're on your way to Land's End today?"

"That's right. Staying in Penzance. Do you ever come to Norway?"

"I've been there a few times. Where do you live?" Rid asked.

"We are in Bergen. Mina and I are in business with her Italian cousins, Tom and Celeste Costa. Tom and I are commercial fisherman. We catch them and clean them. Celeste and Mina sell them every morning in the harbor fish market."

"Sounds like hard work."

"It is, but we enjoy it. How about you?" Harry asked innocently.

"My partner and I recently opened a security consulting firm called Janus International. We're in Rome. Here is our card," Rid said as he handed Bentsen one of their business cards.

"Sounds exciting. Are you on assignment here?" Mina queried.

"No. We are just friends of Lady Joanna."

The Bentsens got up and went over to where Jo was sitting behind a desk. "Would you make up our bill? We are going up to pack and then we will be on our way."

"I have your bill now," Jo replied.

"Good. I'll pay now and we will be on our way."

"Thank you for staying with us."

As the Bentsens were walking up the stairs, Milt Young was coming down. They exchanged greetings. Milt joined Rid at the table.

"I need some coffee," Milt said. Jo heard that and went to get him some. "I thought I heard you talking to the Norwegians."

"Yes. Mostly the 'where do you live and what do you do' kind of stuff."

"What does he do?" Milt wanted to know.

"He's a fisherman from Bergen, according to him. But you know how your antenna goes up about some people?" Rid answered.

"You think he is with New Millennium?"

"Could be. They asked a lot of questions. I gave them our business card, but told them we were not here on assignment."

* * * * *

At that moment the Bentsens were going out the back door and getting in their car. Harry got out his cell phone and called Franz Schwartz at the castle.

"Franz, this is Harry. I got a business card from one of the people here. Says they are in the security consulting business in Rome. He said he was not here on assignment."

"Good, Harry. I'll send Costa to Rome to see what he can find out about them."

"Their names on the card are Ridley Taylor and Milton Young."

"Pretty smug," Franz replied. "That's the names they used on their press credentials for today. But it says Young is with London's *Financial Times,* and Taylor reports for *USA Today.* We'll be ready for them," Franz said as he hung up.

* * * * *

"You think we're walking into a trap?" Rid posed the question.

"I feel certain of it, so let's separate once inside. That way it will be harder for them to keep track of us," Milt suggested.

"Yes, we can use the hand signals we used in Munich. Okay?"

"Okay."

CHAPTER
14

Bodmin Castle—Day 7

Milt and Rid pulled into the parking lot at Bodmin Castle fifteen minutes before the press conference was to begin. There was a line of reporters and photographers waiting to be cleared through security. In addition to the walkthrough metal detector, security was hand searching all bags and making certain each camera could take a picture.

"Looks like they're being thorough, Milt."

"Yeah. We better leave our guns in the car. And you probably should leave the recorder here too."

"Why? I bet most of these reporters use tape machines."

"Not as sophisticated as yours. They may confiscate it."

"It's worth a try. Are you carrying that fountain pen from James Bond's arsenal, the one that shoots stun gas?"

"Certainly, Rid. What could be more common at a press conference than a pen."

They passed through security without incident, although when their invitations and credentials were checked, a secret button was depressed to tell Franz Schwartz his special guests had arrived. By the time the pair of former secret agents had reached the main hall, they knew for certain that they had been made. In subtle sign language they exchanged the identifications of their watchers. Ridley signed "later" with his finger. Milt made the traditional "okay" sign.

"Welcome ladies and gentlemen of the press," Sir Dean began. We hope you will get a full understanding of our New Millennium Foundation while you are here. I want to show you a film about our proposal. It has been updated to reflect the comments of world military leaders that were here a short time ago. After the film, I will more fully explain New Millennium and answer all your questions. Then we will take you on a tour so you can see our operation. Now for the film."

The room went dark, a screen dropped from the ceiling, and the movie began. Scenes from prior wars, acts of terrorism, and the horrors of ethnic cleansing filled the screen. After several minutes, a bright sunrise projected on the screen. After a few seconds, the words "new millennium" overlaid the sunrise. Then Sir Dean appeared on the screen to present the idea of privatizing the world's armies into a single peacekeeping force.

"The primary advantage of this proposal is to eliminate the horrors of war and terrorism you saw in this film. Having one large military serving the entire world means there would be no more civil wars, no new Third Reichs, no threat of nuclear or biological attack from third world countries, and no takeover of territories by the present day superpowers. There will, at last, be peace in the Middle East, Bosnia, Northern Ireland, Korea, Sri Lanka, and other hotspots around the world.

"The other major benefit is the cost of running large-scale militaries. We estimate we can cut each country's military budget by up to sixty percent. That will free up hundreds of billions of dollars for domestic programs. National debts could be eliminated. Welfare and retirement systems could be enhanced. There could be universal health care.

"Very simply, we can have a millennium of world peace at less than half of the present economic cost. Now let me show you around the foundation's headquarters."

The brief video tour of the castle showed the large "Peace Room." To Milt and Rid, it looked like any war room in any country, with world maps, computers, and technicians busy in the message center. Then the video showed the outside of the castle with its large microwave and satellite transmitters. The video ended with the picture of the sunrise and the slogan New Millennium = Peace and Prosperity.

Sir Dean returned to the podium. "Let me explain to you where we are. In two weeks, I will make this presentation to the United Nations. First to the Security Council and then to the General Assembly. I have already reviewed it with military leaders from over seventy countries. In fact, the video reflects some of their comments. By getting behind this idea, the press can sway public opinion so that any government leader who doesn't want to relinquish control or power will think twice before voting against the plan. You can play an important role in assuring peace for all time. Now I will take your questions."

A woman rose saying, "I am Lee Dodd from the *Wall Street Journal*. You mentioned control. Doesn't this place too much power in the hands of New Millennium?"

"A very good question. We sensed the same concern. We plan to propose that the Security Council act as an overseeing body which would review our activities on a regular basis, approve senior staff appointments, and review the contract every three years."

"What do you think are your chances of gaining the U.N.'s approval?" asked a correspondent from Paris' *La Monde*.

"We feel right now we have a better than even chance. With your support, that would rise to seventy-five percent favorable."

"Sir Dean, I am with the *Messagero* in Rome. My name is Bruno Sacco. I am seventy-four years old and lived during times of military control in Italy. This seems like a similar case where, in effect, we will have martial law?"

"Not with the governance of the foundation we are proposing. I have already described the supervision by the U.N. In addition we have recruited to our own board of directors, internationally known business people and economic experts. For example, the president of a very large computer software company from the United States is on the board. So is the head of Fiat Italia from your country. The foundation will be a for-profit corporation with each participating country able to buy shares. We also will offer public shares with voting rights to elect directors each year. I think we have established a structure that will work. Next."

"I am Reginald Wright from *The Economist*."

"Delighted to have you here, Sir Reginald," Floyd interjected.

"Thank you. My question relates to the redistribution of the massive military expenditures. Who will be responsible for those decisions?"

"We feel each country should make its own decisions, as each one has different problems. We will ask each country to pay us forty percent of its present military budget. They can then add whatever their liaison costs to work with us. After that, they can decide anything from a new entitlement to reducing taxes."

Milt signaled Rid that all of their questions had been touched upon.

"Now, ladies and gentlemen, for a closer look," Sir Dean offered, "my associates will take you on a tour. Please ask all the questions you like. After the tour, we will gather in the dining room and the terrace for refreshments."

Groups of twenty were divided by their preferred language for a look at the Peace Room, the communications center, the offices and quarters of the permanent staff, and the outside antennas. The tour covered most of what Rid and Milt wanted to see. They also noted the locations of all the security cameras, entries and exits, and large numbers of armed guards. Each was aware of their followers.

Finally, after exiting one of the rooms in the office complex, Rid could see that the members of his group who were behind him had stopped in the doorway and blocked the advance of his tail. He turned down a darkened hall, went around a corner, and came to the employee cafeteria. He stood beside the door and listened to two of the computer technicians.

"I'll be here all night getting caught up on our message intercepts from the CIA. These damn tours sure take a lot of time," one said.

"If they help sell the deal, we won't have to have any more. Once we are in control, you'll have full time for your covert activities," said the other.

Rid started to retreat to where he left his group, but as he rounded the last corner, there was Sir Dean flanked by two armed guards.

"Ridley Taylor, formerly Agent Taylor of the CIA," Floyd said. "It seems you are here under false credentials. What is your purpose?"

"Much less than you think. My government has asked for my opinion on your plan. Actually it looks like it could work."

"But you left your group?"

"And your assigned tail. I wanted some confirmation that all we've seen is on the up and up."

"Did you get it?"

"Not really. I got into a back hallway that led to a cafeteria. There was nothing there, so I started back this way and ran into you."

"Forgive my suspicious nature, but I sense there is more to you than that story. A little time in our dungeon will change your tune."

"Dungeon?" Rid said almost comically.

"The real thing, complete with rack, iron maiden, and a variety of more modern instruments of torture. Guards, take him to the dungeon. I will get Franz to join you there after he picks up his partner, Milt Young."

CHAPTER
15

Bodmin Castle—Day 7

Milt Young was outside observing the routines of the guards and identifying possible places he could get in unseen. He had let his tour group go on ahead. Only his watcher was there. Then he saw Sir Dean and his security chief, Franz Schwartz, come out of the main house and head toward one of the castle's old turrets. He tried to get close enough to hear them, but only caught the words "Taylor," "dungeon," and "talk." Then Sir Dean turned onto the terrace where lunch was to be served. He began to smile and welcome his guests from the press personally.

Milt could sense that Rid was in trouble, so he crossed the courtyard and went into the turret after Schwartz. As soon as he entered, he stepped aside at the top of a winding staircase. He waited until his tail entered the tower and then sprayed him with sleeping gas from his special fountain pen. The guard slumped immediately. Milt caught him to keep him from falling down the stairs. He picked up the guard's automatic and crept down the stairs. Near the bottom he saw an open door. Peering inside, he was amazed to see a full-fledged medieval torture chamber. In the middle of the room, Rid was seated flanked by two armed guards.

They had obviously been waiting for Schwartz, who said, "Mr. Taylor, what are we to do with you? You have left us no alternative but to find your true purpose for being here. We can do this hard or we can do this easy. Tell me now the real reason you are here and you won't experience the variety of tongue loosening devices we have."

"I already told your boss that I was here at the request of the CIA to give them my opinion of New Millennium's proposal. I thought the concept was good and was prepared to give a positive report. But now, seeing this room and your paranoia about my efforts leads me to think there must be more to this place than meets the eye."

"We'll do it the hard way then. Men, strap him to the rack."

The guards laid down their weapons and began to drag Rid toward the rack.

"Not so fast!" Milt said as he stepped into the room. "The three of you go over and get in that cell. I'll take your weapon," he said to Schwartz.

Rid helped lock the trio in the cell. He then retrieved the guards Uzis and the security chief's Luger. "Thanks Milt. I thought you might come."

"No time for celebration, Rid. Let's get the hell out of here."

They climbed the steps, hugged the walls of the courtyard, and put down the weapons as they entered the terrace where everyone was consuming food and wine. They walked nonchalantly through the crowd with Sir Dean glaring at them. They figured he wouldn't try anything in front of every front page or nightly news anchor in the world. They waited a moment until some of the guests began to leave. They walked out with them, jumped in their car and sped away.

"We have to warn Jo," Rid said. "They'll be coming after us."

"No doubt. We better get her and get out of here."

"We could drive to London and hole up in one of MI6's safe houses. Your former outfit has such things, right Milt?"

"We've got them. There is one a lot closer than London in the village of Chewton Glenn."

They raced into Ruth's Place and told Lady Jo to quickly pack.

"They are after us. We've got to get out of here," Rid shouted.

Jo ran upstairs, threw some things in her suitcase, went down to the kitchen to turn off the stove, and put a "closed" sign in the front door. The other two had retrieved their bags and all three raced to the car. As they were leaving the parking lot, a four-wheel drive Land Rover screeched around the curve and narrowly missed them. Milt turned their car the other way and pushed the accelerator to the floor. As they were entering the village of Bodmin Moor, the Land Rover had caught up with them. The lack of traffic in town allowed them to get through Bodmin without incident. Just outside of town, they turned and entered the Bodmin Moor National Park, an area of peat bogs, marshlands, and quicksand.

They tried to keep their car on the road. The Land Rover kept ramming them in the rear.

"Can you get a shot at them, Rid?"

"I think so," he replied as he retrieved his weapon from under the seat.

Rid turned, put his hand out the window and began firing at their pursuers. They quickly returned fire.

"Get down, Jo!" She dropped to the floor.

The battle continued with the vehicles now side by side. The Rover had pulled even on Rid's passenger side. Just as they were coming to a small bridge, Rid shot the driver in the head. The Land Rover jerked hard to the right and flew off the bridge into a bog.

"That should bog them down," Rid quipped.

"Enough of that," Jo said. "Let's get out of here. I need to find a phone to call my caretaker."

"Okay," Milt said, "but only tell him you'll be out of town a few days. Don't say where."

They drove the back roads up through Devonshire, stopping near Exeter for Jo to make her call. They stayed off the motorways the rest of the way to the safe house in Chewton Glenn. With the car in the garage, they entered the house.

"You need to report what we saw to MI6, Milt."

"We have a scrambler phone here. I'll call now."

"Tell them to relay the information to Bryan Roberts at the CIA. I'll call him later. Tell them to recommend against New Millennium's proposal."

"Okay."

"What happens next?" Jo asked.

"We need new identities, new passports, and money so we can get the hell out of England. They should be able to supply all those things here."

"Now that we're safe, tell me what happened at the castle."

Rid described the press conference, his capture, Milt's rescue, and their race to her manor house. "You know the rest. Something very sinister is going on in that place."

"I knew it," she said.

Milt returned to the room. "I gave them a full report and told them to veto the proposal. They said that might not be possible. There is too much political pressure to improve the world's economy. They still think the Security Council can keep control. They also said they would contact Bryan for you."

"Good. We need new identities," Rid said.

"Way ahead of you. Jeremy Martin is sending them by courier tonight."

"Let's get some rest."

While they were trying to sleep after the excitement of the day, one of New Millennium's listeners was working on descrambling the call to MI6. In a matter of hours he would discover where the two spies had gone.

CHAPTER
16

Chewton Glenn—Day 8

Harry Bentsen returned from Penzance a day early when he heard about the problems with Taylor and Young at the press conference. He was the chief of New Millennium's communication room and he wanted to personally supervise locating the pair. His staff was working on several coded and scrambled messages.

"Wake me up if you get anything on Young or Taylor," he instructed them at midnight.

At 4:30 A.M., one of his aides woke him saying, "We've got them. Young made a call to MI6 from a place called Chewton Glenn. MI6 is sending new identities for them and for a Lady Joanna."

"She is the owner of the bed and breakfast in town. Let's go wake Franz."

The two of them went to Franz Schwartz's quarters where he greeted the news with enthusiasm.

"If they are waiting on new credentials, they must still be there. I'll tell Sir Dean. Harry, you get four of our guards and get two of the Land Rovers ready."

Harry left with his assistant saying, "There will be a bonus for your work on this."

"Sir Dean," Schwartz said as he touched his sleeping boss, "Sir Dean, we have found them. They are in a MI6 safe house in Chewton Glenn."

"That's where the resort hotel that hosts the croquet tournaments is located," Sir Dean said as he wiped his eyes. "Are they at the hotel?"

"We aren't certain yet. We know it's a safe house. I can call my contact at MI6 to get the location."

"Good. And get a team ready to go. You can be there in two hours."

"The team is already standing by, sir."

"Wait a minute, Franz. They have already told MI6 about what happened here yesterday. This Jeremy Martin told Young it might not be enough to stop the United Kingdom's support for our plan because of economic pressures. Killing them may raise suspicions even higher. Let's just put a watch on them until I know from the prime minister's office the extent of the damage. No reason to compound one blunder with another. Send Tom Costa to cover them."

"He's in Rome trying to find out more about their security consulting firm."

"How about Jim Cranwill?"

"He's here. I'd like to go with him to Chewton Glenn. If we see a chance for a peaceful grab, we'll take it. Otherwise, I'll set it up for Cranwill."

"Okay."

* * * * *

"Good morning, Jo," Rid said. "You look absolutely radiant this morning."

"I don't know why. I couldn't sleep all night. It's my fault you're in this trouble," she responded.

"You didn't create New Millennium, dear. The evil Dean Floyd did. And besides, saving the world is what we're trained to do."

"Right!" yelled Milt from the kitchen where he was pouring coffee. He entered the room carrying three hot cups. "No food in the place. This should help."

"What do we do next?" Jo wanted to know.

"Our courier with our new papers should be here any minute. Then I think we should drive to London to talk the government into not supporting the proposal. It's 7:00 now, so we could be there by noon."

"I agree," added Rid. "We can be much more convincing in person. And you, Jo, can describe the chase and the shootings. They will have to believe something is wrong at New Millennium."

At that moment the two Land Rovers from New Millennium were entering the village of Chewton Glenn. Their contact within MI6 had provided them with the address of the safe house. It was Highfield

Cottage, two kilometers out the old north road. It said Peabody on the post box. Franz decided to take one of the Rovers for himself and Cranwill to do a drive by the cottage. As they did, they saw no sign of life. The cottage sat at a crossroad. Franz pulled around the corner to get a look at the back. There he saw a wisp of smoke from the stovepipe. He radioed the other unit to come up and stop short of the cottage.

"We will wait and watch until 8:30. If there's no activity, we will surround the place and enter the front and rear doors on my signal."

Fortunately for the three inside, the courier from MI6 showed up at 8:15. They took the papers and the keys to his car.

"Our car is in the garage outside," Milt said. "It's pretty well shot up and dented. Will you take it back to Heathrow for us?"

"Certainly," answered the courier. He went into the garage, raised the door, and drove out back, south toward the motorway. He passed the same Land Rover he had seen coming up. He was surprised to see five men come out of the trees and jump into the Rover. Then they did a U-turn and began to follow him. He could see in his rearview mirror they were gaining on him. One of them was talking on the phone.

"It's not them," Harry Bentsen was saying, "it's the courier."

"Let him go," Franz said, "and get back here. I really want these three. They got away from me yesterday. Nobody does that twice to Franz Schwartz."

At that moment, Jo, Milt, and Rid walked out the front door and got in the courier's car. They were out of view from Schwartz who was watching the back. They also went south toward the motorway. A short distance down the road they passed the Rover going the other way.

"Wasn't that Mr. Bentsen?" Jo asked. "The one from my place."

"Yes," replied Milt. "We had a funny feeling about him. We better get rolling. I'm going to take the back road through Salisbury to London."

"How did they find us so quickly? Do you think they have an informant in MI6, Milt?" Rid pondered.

"Probably. I would guess they have one or more in every nation that's preparing to vote on their proposal. They have the equipment needed to eavesdrop on phone conversations. They may have recorded my call last night. It would take a while but I'm sure they have the experts to descramble the call."

When they reached the motorway, they went through the underpass at the edge of Chewton Glenn and turned left on the country road to Salisbury.

Franz Schwartz and his team were searching the now-empty cottage. There was nothing of interest to be found. He called Sir Dean on his cellular phone to report their quarry was already gone.

"Return here. One of our informants will find them. Keep Cranwill on alert and tell Costa to watch their office in Rome."

"Yes sir," Schwartz said meekly. Then he hung up the phone and said, "Damn!"

CHAPTER
17

London—Day 8

When Jo, Milt, and Rid reached the outskirts of London, they stopped to call Jeremy Martin.

"This is 0021," said Milt to identify the code he was using. "The lady exposed her bosom. We can see it where we used to dine in one hour."

"Right 0021. I'd like to see that."

"He will be there," Milt said to the other two.

They made their way slowly on some of the back streets of London to The Carriage and Four, a pub in St. James Court. It was close to Buckingham Palace and only a short distance from the government offices, including MI6. At 2:00 P.M. Jeremy walked in. His chief, M, was with him.

"Hope you don't mind, Milt, but I thought she should hear it from you."

"Not at all. It's good to see you, Chief."

"You too, Milt. I knew you couldn't stay out of our business very long. Who are your friends?"

"This is Lady Joanna Devon from Devonshire, and I'm certain you have heard of the CIA's number one field operative, Ridley Taylor."

"I have observed your work on a number of occasions, Mr. Taylor. I particularly recall your work in helping to end the Gulf War. But I don't think we've met," she said shaking Rid's hand. "And you, Lady Joanna, it is a pleasure to meet you."

"The pleasure is mine. Please call me Jo. I don't use the title."

"Only if you call me Evelyn. I hate being called M, but these spy types insist on it. Tradition, they say. Now, tell me about your difficulties with New Millennium."

Milt told the story of Rid's and his attendance at the press conference, of Rid's capture and near torture. He gave details of the car chase and of their pursuers showing up early that morning at the safe house in Chewton Glenn.

"They knew the details of every call I made to Jeremy. They have very sophisticated communication interception systems. I called on the scrambler from Chewton Glenn, so they must also have an informant inside your operation who would know the location of the safe house. They are very upset that we got away and may sway the prime minister's recommendation."

"Anything else?" M asked.

"Yes Evelyn," Rid broke in. "I strayed away from my tour group to see if I could discover anything. I came to their employee cafeteria and eavesdropped on a conversation between two of the staff. 'I'll be here all night getting caught up on our message intercepts from the CIA. These damn tours take a lot of time,' one said. The other replied, 'If they help sell the deal, we won't have to have any more. Once we are in control, you'll have full time for your covert activities.'"

"You two are absolutely convinced that Sir Dean has a nefarious plan."

Both of them answered, "Absolutely!"

Milt added, "I'm convinced he intends to take over the world if his proposal succeeds."

"But what about the safeguards we are requesting with oversight by the Security Council?"

"I understand," added Rid, "that the first renewal of the contract is after three years. They claim it will take that long to get ratification by the various holdout countries. If he gets the superpowers first, he wouldn't have to wait three years for his coup d'état. He even calls his effort New Millennium. That's 1 January 2001."

"Very interesting," M said. "I want you to repeat this for the prime minister. I'm scheduled to meet with him at 7:00 tonight. I'll set it up for the three of you to join us at Ten Downing."

"Jeremy says we may be too late to stop the endorsement of the plan," Milt inquired.

"That's my understanding," answered Jeremy.

"This thing has taken on a life of its own. Both in our Parliament and the U.S. Congress there is overwhelming support. They see billions upon billions of pounds available for their pet projects," Evelyn added.

"Perhaps with more time we could get specific evidence of Sir Dean's real plan," mused Rid.

"That's a possibility," M said enthusiastically. "Maybe we can work with the U.S. to delay the vote and send in an expert team to review their systems, sort of a private audit. Corporations do that before any merger."

"I like that idea," said Ridley.

"I am to call my old boss, Bryan Roberts, at the CIA. He is now the deputy director. I can fill him in both before and after our meeting with the prime minister tonight."

"Good. Tell him to alert the president. I'm certain the PM will want to call him after our meeting."

"All right. But don't forget, New Millennium may be listening. I'd have your offices checked for bugs."

"I already made a mental note to do that as well as look for a mole among my senior staff. Jeremy, you can help with that. Make up a story that we are endorsing the proposal. Make certain it doesn't have the true details. Then give each of my team different versions. We'll see which one gets fed back to us."

"Yes, M."

"Like I said, Joanna, they all do it."

"A sign of respect as I see it, Evelyn. I'll look forward to my first visit at Ten Downing tonight," Joanna replied.

"Not as exciting as you would think. Too many problems all the time. And this new one is a real brain buster," the Chief of MI6 said as she rose and left the pub.

CHAPTER
18

Washington—Day 8

It was 11:00 A.M. in Washington when the CIA's deputy director, Bryan Roberts, picked up his red telephone. The phone was a key link to all U.S. embassies worldwide. They used a dedicated satellite for transmission and changed the scramble codes twice each day. When a call came, their computer descrambled the message, so it was just like talking on the phone.

"Hi, Bryan, it's Rid. I have more on New Millennium."

"Let's hear it. I'll turn on my recorder."

Ridley gave a full account of the visit to the castle, the conversation he overheard, the dungeon with its threat of torture, the escape, the car chase, and the shootings. "Not real peaceful for an avowed pacifist, huh?"

"I'll say. Then what happened?"

Rid went on to tell him about their tracing them to MI6's safe house in Chewton Glenn and their suspicions about New Millennium's communications capabilities. "They probably are capturing this transmission."

"They will never break this code as it changes every twelve hours."

"Don't be too surprised. They have access to all of MI6 and probably have someone inside there at Langley."

"I'll order a security audit," Bryan replied.

"The big reason for my call is that England's Prime Minister, Tony Blair, plans to call President Clinton after we meet with him tonight. We are meeting at 7:00 P.M. here, which is two this afternoon where you are. We are going to propose a thirty-day moratorium on the U.N. vote. That will give time for a detailed review of their operation by an expert U.N. team. We think Blair will agree. That will be the purpose of his call to Clinton."

"I'll see that the president is alerted. Thanks for the info, Rid. Say, how goes the business with Janus?"

"We have our first case. In fact it was our case that led us to New Millennium. We have been hired by Lady Joanna Devon from Devonshire to find a treasure lost in 1188 during the Third Crusade. That's why I asked you for those satellite photos of the Camargue."

"It can't still be there after eight hundred years."

"Maybe not, but we want to look anyway. Lady Jo is a real dish."

"What's the tie-in to New Millennium?"

"Jo's family owned Bodmin Castle before that crusade. We believe the treasure chest contains a royal decree from King Richard the Lionhearted deeding the castle and surrounding lands to her family forever. Bodmin is now Sir Dean's and serves as New Millennium's nerve center and headquarters."

"So if you find the chest, and the decree is intact, you can evict Sir Dean?"

"We can try. It may slow down New Millennium long enough to dig out the truth."

"Okay. Wait a second. I need to call my assistant, Allyson Lee." He covered the phone with his palm and yelled, "Ally, bring me the satellite photo schedule."

She came into the office immediately and handed the schedule to Roberts. Reading down the list he said, "You are in luck, Rid. The metal detecting photos of the Camargue are scheduled for the day after tomorrow."

"That's great. I'm going to stay at our embassy tonight. Let me know the president's reaction to the delay."

"Okay. I'll call on the scrambler at 10:00 tonight, 5:00 P.M. your time. Bye."

"Bye."

After Bryan Roberts hung up the phone he recalled his assistant to his office. "See if you can locate the director. I think he is fishing down in Florida. Also, ask Brendan Howard and Cathy Pageant to come in here."

Brendan took Bryan's place as the head of covert operations when Bryan became the deputy director. Cathy succeeded Brendan as chief of the communications section.

"Sit down," Roberts said as they entered the office. "I have jobs for you."

He played the tape of his conversation with Ridley Taylor. Then he said, "How can you help?"

"I can test our communications to see if they are being intercepted," Cathy replied.

"I can be in touch with Jeremy Martin to get a reading on the British position. I can also put someone on Rid to offer him some protection."

"Good. Those were my thoughts too."

Allyson buzzed Bryan's phone. "The director is out in the Gulf of Mexico fishing and can't be reached at the moment."

"Keep trying. In the meantime, get me the White House, Clinton's chief of staff, Mack McLarty."

When Mack came on the line, Bryan explained the reason for his call.

"You bring that tape here immediately. I'll interrupt the president when you get here. He is planning a news conference this evening to endorse New Millennium's plan with the Security Council oversight. He is getting enormous pressure from Congress to join the program."

"After he hears this and talks to Tony Blair, he may want to delay the news announcement."

"Don't waste time. Get in here."

When Roberts arrived at the White House he was escorted to the side office behind one of the panels of the Oval Office. It served as the president's reading room. Mack was there waiting for Bryan.

"I'll go in and get the president. He's giving a tour of his office to some cub scouts from Illinois." He pushed open the panel and said, "Mr. President, we have an urgent matter to discuss with you."

"I was just about done with these fine young men. The only thing I hadn't shown you was my secret panel. But now my chief of staff has done that for me. Thank you for coming to see me. Scouting is important. Best wishes to each of you."

"Hi Bryan, where's the director?" the president said as he entered the side room.

"In Florida fishing, but this couldn't wait."

"Let's hear it," Clinton ordered.

Roberts played the tape and the president became more agitated as it went on. When it was over, Clinton said, "Son of a bitch. Dean Floyd is leading us to ruin. And he has Congress on his side. All they can see is money to spend to assure their reelection."

"As you heard, sir, the prime minister plans to call you after he meets with Taylor, Young, this Lady Joanna, and the head of MI6. It should be some time after 3:00 this afternoon," Bryan reminded him.

"Yes. Mack, cancel all my appointments after 2:00. Let's plan to delay the press briefing, but don't announce that yet. If Tony and I agree on a thirty-day delay, that's what I'll announce. I need to say something to show our people I'm in charge."

"Yes sir, I'll take care of it."

Roberts left the White House thinking about how politics usually overrides good judgment based on facts. Rushing into an announcement could prove to be a major blunder.

CHAPTER
19

London—Day 8

Milt Young, Ridley Taylor, and Joanna Devon arrived at Ten Downing Street at 6:40 P.M., a full twenty minutes before their scheduled meeting with the prime minister. They were cleared through the security screening and metal detectors. Milt and Rid checked their pistols with the guards. Then they were shown to an anteroom on the second floor where a most efficient receptionist offered them tea. M arrived with Jeremy Martin at five minutes to seven. The receptionist buzzed the prime minister. Almost immediately, Tony Blair opened the door to his office saying, "Please come in, Evelyn. I see you have brought an entourage with you."

"Yes sir," M replied. "You know my assistant, Jeremy Martin. And these are the three I told you about on the phone. This is Ridley Taylor, formally with the CIA, Milt Young, who was one of our best operatives, and Lady Joanna Devon from Bodmin Moor." They shook hands all around.

"Didn't I meet you at a political rally in Exeter, Lady Joanna?" Blair asked.

"Yes sir. The summer before you were elected. But this is my first time here."

"Mostly just an overcrowded set of offices, although the residence rooms are quite comfortable. If you have time when we are done, I'll ask my receptionist, Barbara, to give you the tour."

"I'd like that very much."

"Now, who would like to begin?" the prime minister asked.

"I will, sir," said Jeremy Martin. "I received a call from Milt Young this morning. M and I met with them and heard some very alarming news about Sir Dean Floyd and his New Millennium proposal. We asked them to repeat their story for you."

"All right. What is your story, Mr. Young?"

Milt told the story of their attendance at New Millennium's press briefing and of their ability to intercept and decode top-secret messages. "He also has people in high places throughout your government. We went to a safe house in Chewton Glenn. We told nobody but Jeremy, but they showed up with a small army early the next morning."

"Let me fill in a few gaps, sir," added Rid. "I was apprehended at the castle for straying away from my tour group. Their chief of security already knew who I was. They took me to a real medieval dungeon where they planned to torture out of me the truth of why we were there. Milt came to my rescue and we raced back to town to get Jo. They arrived as we were leaving and chased us through the moor, shooting all the time and trying to bump us off the road. We thought we were safe in Chewton Glenn but, as you heard, they were there the next morning. Not the actions of an honest group that you would put in charge of your country's military."

"Right. Do you have a suggestion of what we should do? Parliament is pushing hard for me to endorse the proposal. We're trying to build in safeguards," Blair quizzed.

M said, "We discussed some options this afternoon. It seems the best thing to do is to set a thirty-day delay in the vote of the U.N. while a full audit can be done on Sir Dean and New Millennium. Mr. Taylor has discussed this with Washington."

"I have President Clinton standing by for a call from you following this meeting, sir," Rid interjected. "But don't be surprised if Sir Dean intercepts the call."

"We have also begun a full internal security review. It will be difficult since Sir Dean is a popular member of our oversight committee of the House of Lords."

"Please stay seated, I will call Clinton now on our dedicated line. It's screened for wiretaps every day." He lifted the handset of a red phone in his desk drawer. He didn't have to dial as it automatically rang in the Oval Office.

"Tony, that you?" Clinton answered.

"Yes Bill, I've just been briefed on new concerns about the privatization of our militaries."

"I've been briefed too. I'm scheduled to have a news conference in five hours at which I was going to announce our support."

"I thought we were going to coordinate our press briefings, Bill?"

"I'm getting enormous pressure from Congress."

"As am I from Parliament. So, what do we do now?"

"The idea that Taylor and Young put forth about a thirty-day delay for an audit sounds good to me, Tony."

"I agree. We could put some of our best communications and security people on the team. We should probably ask Young and Taylor to be part of it to give us a running start."

"Maybe since they're known to New Millennium and have been shot at, they won't want to go back to Sir Dean's castle."

"I'll ask them. Hang on Bill." Tony Blair put the phone on his desk and said, "The president and I would like to have you two on the inspection team if you are willing to return to Bodmin Castle."

Together they answered, "When do we start?"

"As soon as the team is assembled. We will get the delay vote from the Security Council at its meeting the day after tomorrow. The American team could be here by then and our Brits would be ready. Let me tell the president." He picked up the phone and said, "Bill, they are eager to be a part of it."

"Good. Tell them we'll pay them a consulting fee."

"I don't think they care about that, but I'll ask." He put the phone down. "Clinton says we'll pay your consulting fee."

"We'll do it for expenses alone if we can later make a request," Rid replied.

"What's that?" Blair asked.

"Lady Joanna had an ancestor who went on the Third Crusade with Richard the Lionhearted. He lost his treasure in France and died there. We believe the treasure contained a royal decree granting Bodmin Castle and surrounding lands to Jo's family forever. We would want help finding the treasure and, if possible, perfecting the decree."

Blair relayed to Clinton, "You won't believe what they asked for. Just expenses plus a treasure hunt for some treasure lost during King Richard's crusade. That would be about eight hundred years ago."

"In 1188 to be exact," Milt said.

"Sounds impossible, but go ahead and agree," said Clinton. "Now, what about a press conference. I'll hold mine, as scheduled, at 7:00 P.M. our time, to announce our seeking a thirty-day delay."

"That will be midnight here. Just before then I will issue a press release announcing the same thing, so it can hit our morning news."

"Okay," the president said reluctantly, knowing the wire service and satellite news networks would have the story before his announcement. "What time will you release, Tony?"

"Just five minutes before your briefing. You can carry the ball for answering questions."

"Okay. Let's get our press teams on the phone together in ten minutes to draft the text of the joint announcement."

"We'll wait for your call. And we'll start assembling our team of experts. We want to be able to name them at the Security Council meeting."

"We'll have ours in London by the time of the meeting."

"Sounds good, Bill. Let's get on it."

"Okay. Bye," the president said as he hung up the red phone.

"Goodbye," Blair said to no one. Then he turned to the group and relayed, "It is a go. We will jointly announce at midnight that the U.S. and the U.K. will ask for a thirty-day delay in the vote to pursue a due diligence audit of New Millennium."

"You won't be sorry, sir," Evelyn said.

"I'd like M and Jeremy to stay. Are the three of you interested in a short tour?"

"Yes. That would be wonderful," Jo replied.

The prime minister pressed a button on his desk. Barbara, the receptionist, entered the room. Blair said, "Would you give these people the tour of our private quarters. My wife is in the country, so no one will be there."

"Certainly, sir," she answered as she lead the trio out of the office.

* * * * *

At the same moment in Washington, the president was talking with the group that had been assembled for the phone call. The director of the CIA, his assistant Bryan Roberts, Clinton's chief of staff, the chairman of the Senate's Armed Services Committee, chairman of the

Joint Chiefs, and secretary of defense. They had been listening to the private conversation in Clinton's side office. "You all agree?"

"It's the only prudent thing to do," Defense Secretary Cohen replied.

"I hope thirty days is enough time. It will be hard to stall Congress any longer," Senator Warner added.

"I agree with the delay," said the chief of staff, Mack McLarty.

"It's a very good idea," CIA Director John Deutch cast his vote.

"I'm happy we are going to help with Ridley's treasure hunt," Roberts added. "We already agreed to take some satellite photos of the area where they think it was lost."

"Sounds like a real wild goose chase," the president commented.

"True. But the treasure was in a waterproof iron trunk that may have been submerged in the mud of the Camargue."

"We could send a team of our Navy Seals with our new handheld sonar," volunteered the chairman of the Joint Chiefs, Henry Shelton.

"That's great. I'll tell Rid," Roberts answered.

"Mack," the president said to his chief of staff, "get with the press team, have them call the U.K.'s team and work out the wording for my press release. And now, gentlemen, thank you for coming and for your support. We must be very careful not to give our superior military power to some overly ambitious lunatic."

As that group was leaving the Oval Office, Rid, Milt, and Jo were thanking Barbara for the tour.

After they left, the receptionist dialed a number. When the phone was answered, she said, "We need to meet."

CHAPTER
20

When President Clinton stepped to the podium in the East Room of the White House, nearly two-thirds of the assembled press had already seen the satellite news release from Britain's Prime Minister.

"Before I take questions, I have a statement," the president opened. He went on to read the release. He could see a number of them were reading along with him. As he finished reading, he said, "I see several of you have the text of the release. I'll ask my staff to pass our copy out now. To answer your first question, yes, this is a joint release with a copy that was distributed by Prime Minister Blair a few moments ago. The release says that the U.S. and the U.K. will together ask the Security Council for a thirty-day delay in the vote on privatization of the world's militaries. Now, you have questions?"

"Blitzer with CNN, sir. Can you tell us what prompted this request for a delay? We have been assuming the vote for the proposal would pass on Friday."

"Nothing specifically triggered this change. We looked at this as a corporation looks at a merger. We decided we would be derelict in our duty if we didn't execute a full due diligence audit before any vote is taken. This is a monumental step. We want to be sure New Millennium can deliver and the proper oversight mechanism is in place."

"Mr. President," a number of them yelled.

"Yes, Sam," he pointed at Donaldson.

"Mr. President, what about the other members of the Security Council? Don't you already have an agreement that they will act as the oversight?"

"That's in the draft contract, yes. But the details of how that will work still need to be spelled out. I have been on the phone most of the afternoon talking to the leaders of the other council countries. We asked them to provide experts to help with the audit. All but one, Russia, have agreed to support the delay."

"What's Russia's problem?" someone in the back bellowed.

"They think we have enough safeguards now. Just like our Congress and the British Parliament, I'm sure President Putin is getting enormous pressure to turn their military costs toward domestic problems. There is a great deal of infighting going on in his cabinet and he doesn't want to wait even a day, let alone thirty. I plan to talk to him again tomorrow."

"What will be the nature of this due diligence review?" Andrea Mitchell asked.

"It will be a thorough review of everything from the talents of the leadership, to computer systems, communications capabilities, to their methods of operation. We will also review in detail their strategic plan for the first three years."

After a pause, when there were no other questions about the release, another reporter asked the president about another of his affairs. The president answered, "No comment." He turned and left the room. He returned to the Oval Office and picked up the red phone.

"I've been waiting for your call," the prime minister answered. "How did it go?"

"Very well, Tony. It worked out fine for them to have your copy before we started." Clinton then went on to tell Blair of all the questions and how he answered them.

"That was smart not to mention Young or Taylor and the shootings."

"I portrayed it as normal prudent business."

"We'll do the same. I have asked Sir Dean to come to my office tomorrow morning so I can tell him what we plan to do."

"He will have to offer cooperation, Tony, or he would send up a big red flag."

"Right you are, Bill. I plan to tell him that Young and Taylor will be on the team and see what he has to say about their earlier visit. I'll call you at 7:30 your time."

"Make that 6:30, I come in early," Clinton said.

CHAPTER
21

London—Day 9

It was 10:00 A.M. in London when Sir Dean Floyd was shown into the prime minister's office. He had been briefed by his security chief, Franz Schwartz, on his meeting with Blair's receptionist. While they hadn't been able to monitor the calls between the prime minister and President Clinton, Barbara had caught the words "thirty-day delay" and "audit."

"Good morning, Mr. Prime Minister."

"Good morning, Dean. I've asked you here today to enlist your support for a delay of the Security Council vote."

"A delay? What for? Each day costs us over a million pounds. I thought everything was set."

"I need to be frank with you," Blair began. "We are aware of the escapade your security people had with two former intelligence officers who attended your press briefing a few days ago. It raised questions as to whether you have a hidden agenda that you don't want made public."

"That would be Ridley Taylor and Milton Young. An unfortunate incident where my security chief overreacted. I must be candid with you also. We learned of these two coming to our headquarters under false credentials early. We watched them closely while they were there. They were probing in sensitive areas that must remain secret if the whole plan is to succeed."

"What do you mean by that?"

"We have substantial capabilities in capturing internal communications within and between countries. This is necessary if we are to maintain peace. We can't have any country plotting against the plan. We also have recruited military leaders from around the world to be our liaisons. And we have friends in most central governments."

"Spies, you mean?"

"Yes sir. An important part of any successful armed force."

"Dean, we plan to use the thirty-day delay to do a full audit of your systems and capabilities. We expect complete cooperation or the proposal will fail."

"You shall have it. Just make sure all of the examination team have top secret clearance."

"They will. We also have asked Young and Taylor to be on the team in order to get a quick start."

"That is fine with me, Tony. I will personally apologize for the incident and show them whatever they want now that we know they are sanctioned by you."

"Good. We will have the team assembled here tomorrow. Then they'll be ready to start on Friday after the council meets. You're welcome to come and meet them."

"I guess I won't be making the presentation to the Security Council that day."

"No. We will save that till after the audit."

"Then, I would very much like to meet the members of the team. What time?"

"Two P.M. in the Lords' Conference Room. That's near your office, I believe."

"Yes, just down the hall. I'll be there."

Tony Blair waited until 11:30 to call Bill Clinton. "He accepted our terms quite willingly."

"What did he say about Taylor and your man?"

"They thought they were clandestine spies, not working for us. He promises to give them full cooperation."

"That's great, Tony. You're a hell of a salesman."

"Thanks, Bill. Keep in touch."

"I will. Bye."

"Barbara, get M and the people she had here yesterday to meet me for lunch at the Military Club. And get our U.N. Ambassador in New *York* on the phone."

Chapter
22

Sir Dean was waiting in the hall outside the House of Lords Conference Room when Ridley and Milt arrived.

"May I see you two in private for a moment? My office is right down there."

They followed him down the hall and took seats facing his desk. Sir Dean started to apologize for the incident at Bodmin Castle.

"We've already been briefed by the prime minister on your explanation that we were spies," Rid said.

"It's true. We knew from our communications monitoring that you were going to come under false credentials. We had you watched and could tell you were probing our security. We also had learned you operate a private security firm in Rome. We couldn't be certain whom you were working for, but like any good military, we planned to find the truth. We could only figure you were there for some covert purpose. Perhaps we overreacted, but we probably would do the same again in similar circumstances."

"What about the shootings? Your people were not trying to miss," Milt suggested.

"It was you who brandished the gun first. My security force is made up of former commandos and green berets. They react to force with force."

"And the medieval torture chamber?" Rid continued the quiz.

"It came with the castle. We thought just a look at those devices would loosen most tongues. For a professional like you, we would have used more modern techniques."

"Okay. Apology accepted," Milt said. "Will we now be given full access to your operation?"

"Yes. Now that we know you are a part of the team who will audit New Millennium, we will give you everything you want. We really have nothing to hide from people with top-secret clearances. Understand, please, that we do have our own clandestine operations. If we are going to keep peace in the world, we need the most comprehensive spy and communications networks ever assembled. So you will see it all and you can answer the question yourselves as to whether it's necessary."

"I'm sure it will prove to be," Rid said as he stood up. "Now, we need to get to the meeting."

The three of them went down to the conference room. M was at the front table and motioned them all to join her. Then she said to the team, "Welcome! You have been selected for a most important assignment. One that world peace in the next century depends upon. You will be doing a full due diligence audit of New Millennium Corporation. Before proceeding, I'd like to introduce the head of New Millennium, Sir Dean Floyd. Sir Dean, would you like to say a few words?"

"Yes. Thank you, Evelyn. Let me add my welcome to each of you and give you all my assurance that we will provide you with whatever it is you want to review. We only ask that you maintain an attitude of top secrecy and see that your reports go only to those who need to see them."

"Thank you, Sir Dean," M went on. "Next let me introduce Mr. Milton Young, formerly with my MI6 and Mr. Ridley Taylor who was in the field with the CIA."

They rose to wave. They each knew a number of the team's members.

Rid spoke. "We look forward to working with each of you. After a vote later today by the Security Council to sanction this audit, we will be adding team members from the other council countries. M, she likes to be called Evelyn, will act as our leader. Today we need to assemble a list of what we would like to review so Sir Dean can make preparations for our visit. You should plan to be at Bodmin Castle by tomorrow evening."

Sir Dean said, "Let me interrupt for a moment. We have some empty barracks that you can use as living quarters. We're set up for housing and feeding a force of five hundred men after we are in business. And I think you will find the food good."

"Thank you!" Milt replied. "Rid and I have visited New Millennium. We were under false credentials and were caught very quickly at trying to see what will be open to you. They thought we were spies or rivals and treated us as such. We have cleared the air on that concern, but I want you all to beware of the castle's dungeon. It's something right out of one of Dante's books."

They all laughed.

"Maybe Sir Dean will give us a tour."

"I'll do better than that. I'll let you all try the toys on each other."

They all laughed again.

"Enough of this banter," M said, "although it is good to see the three of you joking with each other. Now, just down the hall to the left are four smaller meeting rooms. They have placards outside, each one showing four specialties we envision for the review. Here is a printed list with your personal assignments. If you feel you have been misplaced, please stay a moment when we break up and talk to me. The four sub teams are: organization and finance for those of you who are accountants or management consultants, communications for that specialty, computer systems which is self-explanatory, and covert operations, which will be led by Bryan Roberts, deputy director of the CIA. He will be here later today. Are there any questions before we divide into our groups?"

"Only one," one of the Americans said. "Where is Bodmin Castle and how do we get there?"

"Good. I forgot to announce that we are adding two special cars for you onto the 2:00 P.M. train from London's Paddington Station on the main line to Penzance."

"We will have transportation to meet you at the station in Exeter," Sir Dean added.

Each group went to their respective rooms to begin drafting a list of inquiries. All of them felt the awesome responsibility of deciding if the world's military power should be turned over to a private firm. They thought that Sir Dean was a likeable sort and he was very hospitable. But they couldn't put their finger on what it was about him that made them feel uneasy.

CHAPTER
23

London—Day 10

Bryan Roberts arrived at the House of Lords just before 5:00 P.M. The teams had been working for nearly three hours without a break. Bryan first met with M, Rid, Milt, and Jeremy Martin who had been filling in for him in directing the covert operations team.

"How's it going?" he asked.

"To my view, it is progressing well," answered Evelyn. "I have been going from room to room to observe. They really dug in to their assignments. The biggest conglomerate would love to have an acquisition team like this."

"That's good, because this will surely be the world's largest divestiture," Bryan replied. "How about you three. Is Sir Dean cooperating?"

"He's done a complete about face," said Rid. "Since we caught him with his pants down over our escapade, he's decided to play it that covert activities are a vital part of any military operation."

"Yes," added Milt, "but I still don't trust him. He has a hidden agenda somewhere."

"I agree," M spoke up, "and it is up to the three of you to find the truth. In order to squelch the proposal, we'll need solid evidence of his secret plan."

"We'll do our best," they answered.

"I've booked myself into Dukes Hotel," Bryan said. "Isn't that where you always stayed, Rid?"

"We're there now."

"Let's plan on dinner in my suite tonight. We can go over and edit the four teams' questions to eliminate duplicate effort and to be sure we're probing what we want."

"That's a good idea," Rid replied. "Our client, Lady Joanna, is also staying there and should join us."

"In fact, we should use her place in Bodmin Town as our headquarters. She has a bed and breakfast manor house there with four guest apartments," Milt suggested.

"Our conversations would be more secure," quipped Rid.

"Good idea. The U.S. and U.K. are funding the audit. Let's see if we can't rent her whole place for the month. Rid, Milt, and I will take three of the rooms. We'll hold the fourth for you, Evelyn, if you plan to visit the site."

"I do plan to come at least once each week," she said.

"Jeremy, I want you and the other team leaders to stay with your teams at the castle. They must have officer quarters in their barracks. But, I want you and the others to meet with us at our place every other day to discuss progress on the assignment."

"I'll set it up with the other team leaders. We'll draw up a schedule. I can bring it to your hotel along with the final list of questions this evening," Jeremy offered.

"I have a state dinner tonight," M said. "I would like to have Jeremy participate in your review."

"We welcome that. Plan to come to my room at 7:30, Jeremy. What do you drink?"

"I'm a true Englishman. Bombay Gin neat is my beverage of choice."

"Me too," said Milt.

"Not me," Rid broke in. "I'm American so I drink bourbon with lots of ice."

"What about Lady Joanna?" Bryan asked.

"Chardonnay or champagne for her. And don't call her Lady Joanna; she likes plain Jo."

"Sounds like a nice woman. I detect a certain air about your relationship with her, Rid."

"Oh, I can tell you they are a real item," Milt interjected. "I've had to play chaperone to them all week."

"She is beautiful, Bryan. I have been a complete gentleman. If anything I would like to pursue a long-term relationship with her," Rid explained.

"You don't have to explain your actions to me. Just be sure it doesn't interfere with your assignment. What you do after midnight, one, two, three, or whenever we break for the night is your business. Do I understand that she has employed the two of you to find a lost treasure from the crusades?"

"That's right. Her ancestor lost it in France during the Third Crusade. We think it may still be in the muck of the Camargue," Milt said.

"Rid told me about it and I did ask our satellite surveillance people to get some pictures. Actually, they are taking them today. I'll have them brought by courier tomorrow. The navy also offered a team of Seals, their best underwater experts, to assist in the search."

"That's great. I think we should start the search as soon as possible and not wait the thirty days of the audit. Perhaps Milt or I can go there for two or three days next week. If we find this treasure, we believe it contains a royal decree from King Richard the Lionhearted proclaiming that Bodmin Castle and its lands belong to Jo. That would certainly stop New Millennium for quite a while. They would have to move and redo all their systems. It could buy us more time."

"Okay, Rid, plan to go after our initial review session. Anything else?"

There was silence so they decided to return to the hotel. Jeremy stayed to wrap up the work of the teams.

CHAPTER 24

England—Day 11

The dinner and review session in Bryan Roberts's room that evening was very productive. Jo and Bryan hit it off well. Bryan was an imposing character. A former football player at Howard University, he was six and a half feet tall, weighed about 280 pounds, and was handsome, black, and good natured. The New York Giants drafted him in round six, but he decided to go to Georgetown University's Law School instead. It was there he was recruited into the CIA.

Jo was very curious about American football and Bryan was happy to explain the game. He was Rid's director of field operations and they were good friends. Bryan had risen rapidly at the agency. After fifteen years, at age thirty-nine, he became the youngest deputy director ever.

At the close of their session, they asked Jeremy to set up another meeting of all team members for 10:00 the next morning.

"We'll have to meet in the conference room at MI6," he said. "The House of Lords is in session tomorrow."

"That's fine. Milt will bring us. You get the word to the other team leaders. And would you have this consolidated copy of the question list retyped and enough copies made. I'll want to fax one to the president and to my director."

"M will want one and she will provide one to the prime minister."

Once the copies had been made and faxed, the fax machine at Bodmin Castle sprang to life with a copy from the PM's receptionist, Barbara. Sir Dean called Harry Bentsen and asked him to get his top echelon together at 10:00 A.M. to review the list.

Almost question for question they were being reviewed at MI6 by the team. After the review, Bryan gave them an inspirational pep talk about the importance of their mission.

Following another retype, copies of the final list were made. Faxes were sent again to the White House and Langley in Washington, to Ten Downing, and upstairs to M.

"We should also send a copy to Sir Dean, so he can prepare for our arrival," Milt said.

"Somehow, I suspect he is already prepared," mocked Rid.

Jeremy reminded the team to be at Paddington Station for the special train at 2:00 P.M. Bryan and Milt were to follow Rid and Jo in two cars. They felt they would need cars at Bodmin Moor.

Just before they broke up, an incoming fax was handed to Jeremy. It was from Sir Dean saying, "Thank you for the list of inquiries. We are prepared to give you every cooperation. We understand your train will arrive at Exeter at 6:38. We will be there with buses. I am planning a welcome reception for the team this evening upon arrival at the castle. I hope all of you will come."

"How nice!" Milt scoffed.

"We'll get to see our friend Franz Schwartz again," echoed Rid. "Let's hope he is more friendly than the last time."

"Does Floyd know you are staying at the manor house?" Jo asked.

"Yes. I sent him a room list yesterday by team, identifying the leaders," Jeremy said. "I told him you would be staying at Ruth's Place."

"Good," Bryan answered. "We'll see you tonight, Jeremy, at the castle."

"No matter how conciliatory he seems, each of you be wary of our host. I can tell you that from experience," Rid said as he rose from the table.

"Amen to that," Milt offered as a benediction.

CHAPTER
25

Bodmin Moor—Day 11

Bryan, Ridley, and Milt went back to Dukes Hotel to pick up Joanna and the two rental cars they had arranged. They were on their way about an hour and a half before the team was to leave London. They wanted enough time to get settled at Ruth's Place before they went to the reception at the castle. When they arrived at Jo's inn, her caretaker was there to meet them.

"The phone company people were here this morning. Said you had ordered two additional lines," he said.

"Not me," she replied. "Did any of you order them?"

"It's our friend, Sir Dean, at work," Rid stated.

"We may actually need more lines," Milt suggested.

"Yes. If we can identify the new ones we can use them for simple reports that are given to New Millennium anyway. And, if necessary, we can use them to give Sir Dean some misinformation," Bryan added.

"Let's let the lines stay," Rid continued. "Let's also check all the lines and the whole house for bugs."

They spent the next hour going over the entire manor house, which yielded nineteen different listening devices. They left them in place, but put identifiers on them. They agreed to check every day and to use care in their conversations whenever they were near one of the bugs. They would hold their private conversations outside.

"That Norwegian couple, the Bentsens, came by earlier," the caretaker told Jo. "I told them you were booked solid, like you said, for the next thirty days."

"Good Henry. We will be full, so I'll need you here every day."

Henry Needham was in his eighties, very good at growing things and fixing small problems. He was a coast watcher during the Second

World War, and suspicious by nature. Each of the three visitors thanked him for alerting them to the new phones.

"Henry," said Bryan, "we want to have you in the employ of our investigative team while we are here. In addition to your regular duties for Joanna, we would like you to keep your eyes and ears open both here and around the village. Report anything out of the ordinary to one of us. We'll pay you an additional thirty pounds a day."

"You can count on me, sir. Thirty pounds. My Peggy will be pleased with that."

The group went to their rooms, unpacked, freshened up, and was ready to go to the castle a little after 7:00. Henry called to report that he had seen two buses go up the lane just moments ago.

"Let the party begin," quipped Milt.

They drove to the castle where a valet in uniform parked their car. Sir Dean had been alerted so he was at the front entrance to greet them.

"You must be Lady Joanna from the manor house," he said. "I know it was your ancestors that built this castle centuries ago. You are welcome here any time."

"It is fun to be here. You have made major improvements, I see."

"Quite," Floyd went on. "We have modernized everything from new double pane windows to air conditioning. It is ideal for our activities. I want New Millennium to be a good neighbor. We consider Bodmin to be our hometown."

"The taxing board will be happy about that."

"They have already been to see us," he joked.

They all laughed.

"Let's join the party," he said as he led them out onto the terrace. "I would like to meet your leaders. From the material you sent, it appears there are four different teams."

"That's right, Sir Dean," Rid spoke up. "Let me outline our organization for you. Bryan Roberts, who you just met at the door, is our overall leader on site. Bryan is the deputy director of the CIA in Washington. He also leads the covert operations team, which includes Milt and me."

"Welcome again, Mr. Roberts. I am certain we will get along well."

"As long as you are open to our inquiries, we certainly will."

"Milt Young, and I, you have already met. We are glad we had a chance to clear the air the other day in London."

"Me too. I have instructed my chief of security, Franz Schwartz, to give you full cooperation."

"M, from MI6, is our chief executive. She plans to be here at least once a week for a review session. I know she will want to visit with you. Jeremy Martin is her representative here."

"I've known Evelyn for years, and I have met Martin."

Jeremy brought the three other team leaders over to where the group was standing. "Sir Dean, let me introduce our other team leaders. This is Keith Wright who will lead the organization and finance group, Arthur Cragoe who leads the computer systems team, and David Vanselow who is our communications specialist."

"Nice to meet each of you. With the expertise you all have, this is like getting a free management review of our operations. I will be very interested in your findings and welcome any suggestions you have for improvements."

"With the favorable vote for the delay last night, we expect some or all of the other Security Council nations to send additions to the teams. We'll keep you up to date on any additions."

"Please pass that information on to Schwartz. He will keep the room list and handle any problems members of the team may have."

Bryan said, "We plan to meet with this group of leaders every other evening at Ruth's Place. After each meeting, we will meet with you at 8:00 the next morning so we can each know where we stand. We can also discuss any problems. We will also meet with M each time she comes."

"A good plan. I know we can prove to you the merits of our proposal. Now, let's get something to eat."

CHAPTER
26

Bodmin Castle—Day 12

Even though it was Saturday morning, the morning alarm bell rang in all the barracks at 6:00 A.M. There were calisthenics at 6:15 for thirty minutes, then a half hour for cleanup and making the bed. Breakfast was served at 6:45. About half the team participated in the exercises. The other half tried to get a little more sleep to overcome the party from the night before.

They went to their respective rooms to begin work at 8:00 A.M. Each team found a mountain of material waiting for them. It looked like thirty days would not be enough time. They separated the work by the team members' expertise and dug in earnestly.

Bryan, Rid, and Milt arrived at 7:50. Franz Schwartz was at the door to meet them. "I'm sorry I didn't get a chance to talk to you last evening. I was busy preparing the accommodations for your team. I did want to apologize for my actions during your last visit. It was harsh, but you were acting very strange and we knew you had false papers. Perhaps as professionals, you would do the same."

"Perhaps," Rid answered.

"And you are Mr. Roberts of the CIA," Schwartz said to Bryan.

"That's right. Let's get to work."

Franz led them to a small conference room next door to Sir Dean's office. There they found spiral bound books labeled "strategic plan," with each book adding its own specialty, such as overall plan, marketing, personnel policy, organization, timeline, technology, communications, budget, and covert operations.

"Have you given copies of these plans to the other teams?" Bryan asked.

"Only selectively. We gave the technology plan to Mr. Cragoe, the budget to Mr. Wright, and communications to Mr. Vanselow."

"Good. Then we'll start with the others, with the overall plan being first. As we read it, will you gather the personnel files on each of your employees? We'll want to look at those and interview a random sample of them. That should give us a feel for the organization."

"You want the files on the people here at Bodmin, right?"

"Do you have employees in other places?"

"No. Only contract providers of information. We are reluctant to publish that list of secret assets."

"We won't need that for now, but may want to discuss it with you and Sir Dean later."

Schwartz left to get the files. Bryan said, "Rid, you read the covert op book and write down all your questions. Milt, you do the same for the timeline, and I'll work on the overall plan. We can save the others till later."

"What was the idea behind wanting to interview employees?" Milt wanted to know.

"You never know what they might tell us, particularly if we get an unhappy one. At the very least we'll get the office scuttlebutt."

"That's a good idea," both Milt and Rid agreed.

They sat down to read. They became so engrossed in their work they were surprised when Franz, with a pushcart full of files, entered the room and announced, "It's 12:30, time for lunch."

Over lunch, the leaders of the team sat at a large round table Sir Dean had reserved for them. Dean was already there. "I realize there will be days when you may want to work through lunch or eat with your respective teams. Today, though, I wanted a quick check to see if you have everything you need."

Bryan said, "We're all right for now. We may want to discuss your network assets later."

Rid added, "Perhaps we can do that by position instead of names."

"I'm working on the timeline. The 1 January 2001 keeps coming up as a significant date. I'd like to know why," Milt queried.

Wright stated, "Our financial team is just getting started. We'll have a number of requests later."

Cragoe informed him in turn, "You've given us good documentation on your systems. In addition, we would like to see samples of all the output of your programs. Also, I would like to see the internal computer code. I can read that to see if it matches the documentation."

"We should tour your communications areas to get a feel for how large and complex they are," Vanselow remarked.

Jeremy mentioned, "I think I could be of more help to M if I could move around among the teams to view their progress."

"Okay," Sir Dean began. "Bryan and Rid, we will discuss our network of operatives with you. I ask that no notes be taken. Milt, to answer your question, I named this enterprise New Millennium and set the date of January 1, 2001 as a challenge to myself and everyone connected to the project to get it done. It's not a hard and fast date, but we still see it as doable. Keith, I know your task of dealing with the numbers is the most difficult. We will provide what you want. For you Art, I am impressed that you can read that gobbledygook the computer's operating system reads as code. You may even find some bugs for us to correct. David, we'll arrange a tour of our communications installation right after lunch. And Jeremy, your request makes sense to me, but it is Bryan's call."

"I think it's fine, Jeremy," Bryan said. "You can keep me posted as well. Why don't you take the tour with Vanselow's group this afternoon, then sit in with Cragoe."

"I hope he doesn't expect me to read the code. How does he do that?"

Art responded, "I'm an actuary by training and have designed and built my own computers and their operating systems."

"You really have a talent laden team, Bryan," Sir Dean said as their food was served.

"Thank you, we are here to find out if your team is as talented to handle the world's problems, Sir Dean."

"I'm confident you will find it so. We are an open book to all of you," Sir Dean said with a wide smile.

CHAPTER
27

Bodmin Moor—Day 12

When Milt, Rid, and Bryan returned to Ruth's Place around 7:15 P.M., Jo's caretaker, Henry, was waiting in the yard. He was taking his lookout job very seriously.

"Someone waiting for you inside. Showed up this afternoon. Said he was a courier with something for Mr. Roberts. Said he could only give it to him, so he'd wait."

"Thank you, Henry, I have been expecting him. You're doing a good job," Bryan complimented the old man.

"Enjoy it," he said. "Makes me feel good. Almost young again like when I was a coast watcher."

The three went inside to find the courier was Ken Merrill. Ken had been the CIA station chief in Rome during the Gulf War. He was seriously injured in a gun battle with some Iraqi assassins at the Palermo Airport. He was on disability from the agency, but he still did jobs like this one.

"It's good to see you, Ken," Rid shook his hand.

"That goes double for me," Milt added. He had been stabbed in the stomach during that same operation.

"Make that triple," Bryan hugged Ken. "You look great."

"All because of you, my friend." Bryan had been there when Ken was shot in the chest. He had plugged the hole with his hand while the bullets were zinging around them. It saved his life.

"These the satellite photos of the Camargue?" Milt asked.

"Yes, several straight overhead regular photos of the terrain, such as it is, and heat and metal detector shots on transparencies, so you can overlay them on the photos."

They laid the photos out on the dining room table and began to study them.

"These metal shots show stuff all over the place. Looks like a junkyard," Milt suggested.

Bryan replied, "Our new technology allows us to pinpoint things as small as a pop can. Did you bring the CD-ROM, Ken?"

"Yes, here it is."

"This will help us sort it out. With the photos on disk in our computer, we can zoom in on the various hotspots and should be able to tell their shapes."

"Before we go on, let's get a drink," Rid said, motioning them to follow him and be silent. They picked up Jo in the kitchen where she was fixing their dinner and went out to the backyard. "We ought to know better. We have to assume Sir Dean is listening."

"We didn't say what we're looking for, did we?" Milt wanted to know.

"No," answered Bryan. "So let's come up with a story for Mr. Floyd."

"How about we are looking for a downed satellite. One that is used to jam other signals so they can't be intercepted," Rid offered.

"That's great, Rid. It ought to get him pretty nervous about ruining his spy network. Let's go back in and feed that to him. In the meantime, Milt, you and Ken load the CD-ROM onto the computer and see what you get. Just don't talk."

"I'll finish dinner," Jo said. "We can eat in twenty minutes. Poached salmon, okay?"

"Mmmm," they said as a chorus.

"Set a place for Ken. He's an old friend. Can he use Evelyn's room tonight?" Bryan suggested.

"You're paying for it. Why not use it," she said.

Rid, Ken, and Bryan returned to the dining room. Bryan made a motion to Rid to begin.

"I feel better now that I've had my scotch," he said. "Let's get back to the pictures, Ken. Do we know the shape of the downed satellite we're looking for?"

"Yes, I brought pictures of it too. It's about the size and shape of a small Volkswagen bug. It won't be hard to recognize."

"Even if we find it, can it be put back in service?" Bryan said while smiling and pointing up at the bug in the light fixture.

"I understand the signal jamming unit is easily replaceable. We could have it ready to send back up within two weeks."

"That's great, Ken. Let's go freshen up for dinner. Lady Joanna needs to get in here to set the table," Rid closed the act as they left the room.

* * * * *

At Bodmin Castle, Sir Dean turned to Franz Schwartz and said, "Do you have any idea what that was about?"

"No sir. Our agent in Rome, Tom Costa, reported that Lady Joanna appears to have hired Young and Taylor from their firm, Janus International, to find something."

"We'll, I'm quite certain Lady Joanna didn't lose a jamming satellite. We must know more about this."

Franz sneered, "Perhaps I can get Lady Jo to tell me. I'd enjoy that."

"Not yet, Franz. Not yet."

CHAPTER
28

Bodmin Moor—Day 12

After dinner, Jo cleared the table and cleaned up in the kitchen. The others went for a walk around the manor house grounds.

"Tell us more, Milt, about what you can see from the CD-ROM pictures," Rid asked.

"Like Ken said, it shows all kinds of metal. Everything from what looks like a semi truck to beer cans. It sure would be helpful if we knew the size of the treasure chest."

"I wonder if there is a description in any of Jo's old papers. I could ask her to look tomorrow," Rid volunteered.

"We could also ask Monsignor Corso to see if they have descriptions of other chests from the same era. You would think that many of those who were financing the crusade would have similar chests. I'll call him on my cell phone in the morning," Milt added.

"I think we may have seen a list of weights that were put on Earl Ompree's three ships when they left Exeter. That would be at the abbey in Berchtesgaden," Rid was building their list of possibilities.

"I'll ask Ricardo to call them too," Milt replied.

"We could probably estimate the size, at least the maximum," Bryan interjected into what had been a two-way conversation. "We know it was made of iron so it would be heavy even with nothing in it. You said the earl took things like gold and jewels that could be used for currency. And, supposedly he had the royal decree granting Bodmin Castle to his family forever. An iron box full of gold would be too heavy for two men to carry on board. They could have used a sled with handles and four men. So how big can it be?"

"Sounds like something between a breadbox and a footlocker," Ken put in his thoughts.

"Ken and I will start with those parameters tonight to see how much we can eliminate. If needed, Ken can you stay here tomorrow to finish the task?" Milt said.

"You bet. I haven't had this much fun since I left active duty," Ken said excitedly.

"Okay, let's get at it," Bryan said. "I want to finish studying Millennium's overall plan tonight. You two get to the computer. Remember, no talking. Rid, you better brief Lady Jo out here."

"My thought, exactly," Rid showed his eagerness.

Rid went to the kitchen where he helped finish drying the dishes. Then he said, "Let's take a walk. The moon over the moor is beautiful tonight."

Outside, Rid took her in his arms and kissed her. Her lips were full and responsive. She pressed herself close to him and could feel the heat of his loins. Then he released her and drew back.

"Not yet," he said. "I have exciting news and a job for you tomorrow."

"Just like a man. He gets a girl worked up and then goes to watch some sport show on television."

"This is better than that. We think we can narrow the search for the chest considerably. Milt and Ken are going to work tonight on the computer images to identify only those that are bigger than a breadbox but small enough to be lifted by four men. We are going to ask Ricardo to check the Vatican records to see if they have any drawings of trunks from that era. And we'll ask the monks in Berchtesgaden to see if the old ships' logs listed weights of all the cargo. The more we find out, the better our chance of finding it."

"That is exciting. I guess I'll have to take it as a replacement for sex," she moaned.

"Only till we complete your job, sweetheart!" he said in his best Humphrey Bogart impression. "Seriously, Jo, I have never felt this way before about any woman. I think we are good together and I want us to build a lasting love. I'm very close to saying the 'M' word. And I don't mean Evelyn."

"I am very fond of you, Rid, and agree we could be heading towards a lifelong relationship, so letting it develop slowly is fine with me."

He took her in his arms again and their hearts skipped a beat at the electricity generated by the kiss. They both were excited about the prospects of things to come.

CHAPTER
29

Bodmin Moor—Day 13

Even though it was Sunday, most of the team were at their desks at 8:00. Milt had made his call from the car to Monsignor Corso in Rome who readily agreed to look for information on the probable size of the treasure chest. He would call the abbey and ask the monks to do the same.

As they were nearing the castle, Bryan turned to Rid and asked, "Do you think it's time to deploy the Navy Seals?"

"Milt said Ken could finish narrowing the search today. If the others find any other clues as to size, we could be ready the day after tomorrow."

"Good. Evelyn plans to be here tomorrow night for her first briefing. You need to be here for that. You can plan on leaving the next day to lead the search."

"Okay, Bryan. Where is the team now?"

"They have been deployed on a cruiser of the Mediterranean fleet that is currently at anchor at Marseilles. They'll move tomorrow to the town at the bottom of the delta."

"It's called St. Maries de la Mer," Milt interrupted.

"Yeah, there. They'll put their launch and rafts in the water and meet you there."

"The closest airport is at Marseilles. There is a private field at Arles, which is only thirty kilometers up the Rhone from St. Maries. How about a charter?"

"I'll have an air force plane ready to pick you up at the base in Plymouth that morning. One of the Seals' boats will meet you there."

"Thanks, Bryan. What's our agenda today?"

"We need to finish reading their plans. Then we need to make a list of things to discuss with Sir Dean. We need to meet with him before our report to M tomorrow evening."

"What's your early take on the plan?" Milt asked Bryan.

"I stayed up most of the night reading and rereading parts of it. It is extremely well done. It makes a very good case for their proposal. But, I have this nagging suspicion that the plan can be read two ways. One, the way they want us to read it. And another, by following the exact same plan, they could set themselves up to control the world."

"By the new millennium, 1 January 2001," Rid said as they pulled into the visitor's lot at the castle.

CHAPTER
30

Bodmin Castle—Day 13

They spent the day studying the other sections of the plan. At lunch, they assembled the team leaders.

"I want you all to come to dinner tonight at Ruth's Place. Bring with you a report of your early findings. Jeremy, Rid, Milt, and I will meet with Sir Dean tomorrow morning to get answers. Then, tomorrow evening, M will be at Ruth's to hear your reports."

"I'll be ready," said Dave Vanselow.

"We're just getting started. We have asked for samples of the output of all their computer systems," Art Cragoe said. "They use several different platforms to do their work. Their mainframe drives them all and keeps the data. But we haven't seen the documentation for the subsystems. There even could be a standalone personal computer for secret plans and we wouldn't know it was there."

"We'll ask Sir Dean about that," Bryan replied.

Milt made a circular motion around the room and then touched his ear. "We may already have asked."

Keith Wright said, "We'll be ready tonight. This is a huge undertaking and their financial plan is well thought out. It depends on nearly one hundred percent participation by the United Nations."

"What's the chance of that?" Jeremy asked.

"Not too good without some coercion," Keith responded. "There will be several dictators from the third world countries who won't give up their power base."

"Most terrorist organizations will stay in business. Particularly in those areas where religious or ethnic differences have divided their countries for centuries," Rid stated.

"That's what the barracks you're staying in are for. In the plan I read last night, it calls for a five-hundred-man antiterrorist strike force to be housed here. They would respond immediately to any acts of terrorism."

"Who would be in this group?" Jeremy asked.

"The plan says they will recruit from the militaries where they assume command."

"This is covered in the financial plan as well," Wright began. "Their personnel costs are set at least fifty percent and some as much as one hundred percent higher than their counterparts in the U.S. They also have a bonus system for outstanding performances and a profit sharing program for all."

"Where do I sign?" Rid quipped.

"Actually, I intend to propose that any profits go back to the countries pro rata to their payments to New Millennium," Keith said.

Again Milt motioned to the walls and his ear.

"Put that in your report and we will get a reaction from Sir Dean tomorrow. Now let's get back to work. I'll see you all tonight. Jeremy has one of our cars. He'll bring you." Bryan closed the lunch by bringing his forefinger up to his lips as if to remind them not to talk in the car.

When Bryan, Milt, and Rid left that afternoon, Milt whispered, "Someone has been in the car."

Bryan repeated the silence motion. They talked about football on the way to Jo's house. There they debugged the car, which had both audio transmitters and location tracking devices.

"We need to put a bug in Sir Dean's office to get even," Rid suggested.

"That's a great idea, Rid, let's do it. You figure out how."

CHAPTER
31

Bodmin Moor—Day 13

Jeremy and the team leaders arrived promptly at 6:30. A quick scan of their car revealed the same audio and tracking devices as had been in the other car. They were quickly disabled. The group went to the gazebo that Jo's mother had built at the edge of the moor. They could see vapor rising from the moor and there was a strong smell of peat.

"I asked you to come out here so we could talk without our host listening in. Now, let's summarize where we are and what we want. Art, you said something at noon about not being able to know if you have seen everything. Something about platforms?"

"Yes, a platform is simply any device that can operate either on its own or in conjunction with a host computer. They could be standalone computers, intelligent terminals, printers, networking devices, or any number of things. When they want to use a portion of the mainframe, they dial it up. Thus, when they are not on line, we wouldn't know they are there by looking at the main computer only."

"What should we do about it?" Bryan asked.

"Well, if Sir Dean heard us at lunch, then he knows you are going to ask about it tomorrow. I think we should wait and see how forthright he is in his answer. Then, we should ask for an inventory of all their hardware and we should physically count it."

"Okay, we'll ask him tomorrow. Keith?"

"My written report is here. The thing we are the most impressed by is the magnitude of his proposal. You're talking about a multi-trillion dollar operation when they are up and running. Each country is asked to contribute forty percent of its defense budget, for starters. The percentage can be adjusted under a certain formula. Each country will also maintain a small military to do the liaison and administrative work to keep in touch with New Millennium. All bases, weapons, tanks, planes, and ships are to be under control of Millennium. I assume they would hire the leadership of those facilities to use them as their own. As I said today, they have very liberal pay scales and offer bonuses and profit sharing. I think we should ask that profits above a certain level, say five percent of gross income, be returned as a discount to each country's next payment. Beyond that, we are just getting into the details. We will want to talk to leaders in countries of various sizes and resources to get their estimates of the impact of the proposal on their budgets. We also should see what the economic impact, particularly on defense contractors, would be. If this plan works as designed, they'll need far less of everything. Unemployment would rise to unprecedented levels."

"We need to bring up your last point with M tomorrow night. We will see what Sir Dean has to say about a lid on profits in the morning. David, what about communications?"

"They have the best setup I've ever seen. We believe that they are able to intercept all forms of communication. They have a well-trained staff of cryptologists and must have their own spy satellites. We can check the launch records from all the world's space centers. That would give us a count of what they have up there."

"Why don't we just ask him?" Rid said. "After we're done asking for his profits, he may be willing to tell us more about communications. Remember, Bryan, we want to talk to him about his human assets in our governments too."

"Right. Jeremy, are you making notes? We need to write down all these questions."

"Yes. I have been putting them down."

"Our small group thinks the plan is sound and could mean world peace if done in the cooperative tone of their strategic plan," Bryan started. "We are concerned though, that by following the same plan, New Millennium will become powerful enough to rule the world. We intend to interview a number of Sir Dean's officers and employees to try to find any hidden agendas. Rid suggested that we should bug Sir Dean's office."

"I think it's only fair. We find new bugs everyday. Be careful what you say inside. Do any of you have someone on your team who is expert at this kind of thing?" Rid asked.

"You're in luck," Vanselow answered. "Our communications team includes Louise Downs from Her Majesty's Secret Service. She is one of the world's leading experts on spy paraphernalia. In fact, she has a suitcase full of the stuff here."

"Could you bring her and the suitcase to our conference room at a 7:45 in the morning. We will talk only about your assignment, but we will write questions for her at the same time. What we need is a small transmitter that we can stick under his desk or table. She could write out instructions for that tonight," Bryan ordered. "Sound good to you, Rid?"

"You asked me to figure out how to do this. I'm glad I did it so fast. Louise Downs, huh?"

"She helped train me," Milt said.

"She is tops. Works with our people all the time," Jeremy added.

"Let's break for dinner. Lady Joanna is a good cook. Remember only casual conversation inside." Bryan closed the session with, "Have your reports finalized and typed for our meeting here with M tomorrow evening at six."

* * * * *

As they entered the house and began their small talk, Sir Dean turned to Franz Schwartz and grumbled, "They must have had their meeting outside. They're on to our devices. We need something new."

"How about putting a long range directional microphone with a dish out in the moor. An operator there could record everything."

"Is there any place out there the operator could hide?"

"In a small boat he could lay down below the height of the grasses."

"Do it tonight. I need to know what they filter out when they come to meet with me. I think our best plan is to agree with every demand they make. If it sells the proposal, in a few years it won't matter what we promised," Sir Dean chortled as he waved Franz from his office.

CHAPTER
32

Bodmin Castle—Day 14

Louise Downs and Dave Vanselow were waiting outside the conference room Bryan, Rid, and Milt were using as an office. "I brought along Louise this morning to give you a more complete picture of New Millennium's communications system."

She set her briefcase on the table and removed three small devices. She set them on small note cards in front of the trio. They began to read the instructions on the cards as she spoke. "This installation is extremely well done. I have done audits of NASA's Kennedy and Johnson Space Centers, as well as the Pentagon, but I have never seen an operation this big or this complete."

As she continued to give examples of the equipment and systems, she read the notes the three returned.

Milt wrote, "How is it activated?"

She scribbled, "Voice."

Rid's note read, "What's the range?"

She scrawled, "Twenty yards."

Bryan had two questions. "Do these stick to anything?"

She nodded yes.

"Where's the receiver?"

She took a small thing out of her bag that looked like a telephone answering machine. She wrote, "This works as an answering machine, so it's well disguised. It also records everything any of the three devices pick up for up to three hours of conversation. The tapes are removable and here are ten tapes."

As she wrote the last part of the note, she was saying, "It is my expert opinion that this installation is capable of all that is needed to accomplish New Millennium's plan."

"Thank you, Louise. That is very helpful," Bryan said. "Thanks, Dave."

As they left the room, Sir Dean was sitting at his desk in the next room beaming at the glowing report she had given. Bryan pointed to the other two and their devices. Then he pointed to Sir Dean's office door, as if to say, put them in there. Then he took his device and stuck it under their conference table. That way, if Sir Dean had a meeting there in the evenings, they could pick it up. They walked into Floyd's office.

"Good morning, Sir Dean. Are we too early?" Bryan said with the other two echoing, "Morning."

"You're right on time. I wanted to have our meeting as soon as possible today. I guess I am very curious about what you have found."

"It's still very early in the audit, so it's too soon to make any specific recommendations. We do have some early general opinions, though. In fact, we just finished meeting with members of our communications team. We have on the team one of the world's foremost experts in such systems who gave high praise to your setup."

"Perhaps I'll have to hire her, once we're in business."

Alarms went off in the trio's heads as they hadn't said she was a woman. It was obvious Sir Dean had been listening.

Bryan went on, "We do have some things to discuss and some items to request. First, our computer specialists recognize the complexity of your systems. They talked about such things as distributed processing and platforms and standalone computers. I don't claim to understand any of that, but it boils down to their uncertainty as to whether they will see all the parts."

"I think we have given them all of the systems' documentation."

"They admit it looks complete. They would also like an inventory record for all hardware. They will use it as a cross check to the systems. They want to physically see each piece."

"It will be done. I can tell you now there are no computers here that are not part of the system, except for one. I have a notebook computer in my living quarters. I use it for my personal financial record keeping, my taxes, and my schedule with the House of Lords. I take it back and forth to London with me."

"We'll tell them that they will be given access to all hardware with that one exception."

"Yes, that's fine. They will have the inventory today."

"Next, the financial team is in awe of the magnitude of your plan. They raised two concerns. First are your liberal pay scales, bonuses, and profit sharing plans."

"It's done after very careful consideration and study. We want to hire the very top performers from around the world. With an incentive system we can assure on time and under budget results. The profit sharing program makes them a part of the corporate family we will try to build. I have been thinking recently that the profit sharing funds should be invested in New Millennium stock. That would further tie our workers' loyalty to our mission. Remember the basic proposal is to privatize the world's military. Private enterprise runs on profits and incentives. Democracies with market driven economies have proven this many times."

"One approach to this issue for you to consider is to put a cap on your profits. For instance, it could be set at five percent of gross revenue, which is a very liberal margin. The balance of any profits over that could be a dividend or deduction from the subscribing country's bill for the next year."

"I'm opposed to any limit on profits. As I said, it is the profit motive that will be our driving force. I do like the idea of some system of rebates to the participating countries. Frankly, I hadn't thought about that. Let me see if I can come up with something to accomplish your suggestion. I should be able to have it for you by the end of the week."

"All right, we'll hold on that one. We have a general concern about the economic impact of your plan. There will be millions of people out of work: Military personnel, defense contractors, base closures, service industries to the military, the list goes on and on," Bryan made his case.

"We have thought about that very carefully. It's the reason our motto is New Millennium equals peace and prosperity. The key is to do both. Our hope is that the individual countries will initiate domestic programs to absorb these workers."

"That will take time," Rid said.

"We're prepared to work off the excess people on a gradual basis. Perhaps an early portion of the sixty percent savings can go into retraining and relocation programs."

"This is a concern we will raise to the Security Council," Bryan stated.

"Fair enough. I'll cover it in my presentation."

"Our communications gurus, as I said, are most impressed with your setup. They would like to know the location and purpose of all the satellites you have in space."

"That is secret information. I'd like it only seen by those who need that information."

"We can do that. When can they see it?"

"Later today. Perhaps they can come here or your conference room. We better control the release that way. I will meet with them."

"Okay. We know another very sensitive area is your human assets among our various governments. How do you think we should proceed on this issue?"

"I am having a list made of functions for these people. They are not identified by name or country. When we next meet, I will share that list with you and try to answer your questions."

"That should work. I believe that's all of our early questions," Bryan went on. "Thank you for being so open and cooperative."

"Happy to do it. It's important to my dream of a world at peace."

"Oh, one more thing. Milt and I would like to start interviewing some of your personnel tomorrow. Should we contact them directly?"

"No. I'll have Franz Schwartz available to bring whomever you want to your room. What kinds of things will you ask them?"

"Simple things really. Like background, education, specialties, hobbies, and such. What things do they read. What's their opinion on the chance for success for New Millennium."

"That should demonstrate the quality we have here. I particularly like your question about reading preferences. I am a voracious reader. I once heard a well-known lecturer on success say, 'If you are to achieve greatness, then you must stand on the shoulders of giants.' He went on to promote the reading of biographies of famous people. I have a large collection here," he said pointing to the far wall that had bookshelves from floor to ceiling, complete with the rolling ladder for retrieving the ones higher up.

"May we look?" Milt asked.

"Certainly." He rose and led them to the shelves. "This is the biography section."

There were books about famous people from all walks of life, but the most frequent were about conquerors and military leaders: Alexander the Great, Genghis Kahn, Napoleon, Hannibal, Peter the Great, Attila, as well as Lincoln, Churchill, Eisenhower, MacArthur, Montgomery. There was a book on Saddam Hussein. They had pulled a few off the shelves, leafed through them, and put them back.

They said their goodbyes and returned to their conference room. There while they discussed the meeting, noting how well it went, Rid and Milt wrote notes.

Milt's said, "I put mine under the chair I was in."

Rid's note said, "I put mine on the back of the book on Lincoln. That's one I doubt he consults very often."

When they left that afternoon for their meeting with M, they took the tape of conversations with them. They loaded another in its place.

After they got to Jo's, Rid said, "I sure would like to get at that personal computer Sir Dean keeps in his room."

"Me too," added Milt. "Can we do a little second story work, boss?"

"Be my guest. I'll clear it with Evelyn tonight," Bryan said.

Henry met them at the door. "Woman arrived about an hour ago. Lady Joanna showed her to her room."

"That's good, Henry. Anything else?" Bryan asked.

"There was some hunters out on the moor today. But I didn't hear any shooting."

"Hmmm. We better check that out," Rid offered.

"Yes, you two do that. I'll go talk to Evelyn and brief her on what she will hear this evening. The public version, of course."

"We better not use the gazebo tonight. We can debug the library if you like, Bryan."

"Good idea. Everyone else will be here at 7:00."

After changing clothes, Milt got his Walther PPK revolver and went out onto the moor. He circled wide and came back toward the gazebo. He was moving silently as dusk was settling in. By the twilight he could see the parabola of a directional microphone sticking up above the weeds. He approached it very cautiously. As he reached the spot, he saw a small punt in the water by the microphone. There was a man lying in the boat.

Milt stepped out of the reeds saying, "Put up your hands. Leave your gun there in the boat. Now you get out of here and go back and tell Sir Dean or Schwartz that all this distrust must end. I'll talk to Sir Dean myself in the morning to make sure you did."

Milt disabled the microphone and returned to the house. Bryan, Evelyn, Rid, and Jo were in the library.

Rid said, "I've debugged this room. We should be okay."

"I found a visitor in the moor that had a parabola mike. It doesn't work any more and he is on his way to tell Sir Dean to stop with the bugging."

"Let's ask him to call a truce in the eavesdropping," Bryan said. "I'll do that tomorrow. Now, let's have a drink while we wait for the others."

"What's for dinner, Jo?" Milt wanted to know.

"I asked Evelyn what she would like. She chose lamb chops and cottage fried potatoes."

"Sounds good," Rid said even though he was not fond of lamb. "I hope the group gets here on time."

CHAPTER
33

Bodmin Moor—Day 14

The meeting with M went very well. Each of the team leaders gave her a written report with a concise oral summary. She had nothing but praise for their efforts. "It is astonishing to me," she said, "how far you have come in just a few days. Do you feel you will finish ahead of the thirty-day deadline?"

"The devil is always in the details," Art Cragoe answered. "The more we dig into their systems, the slower it will go."

Then Bryan reported on their meeting with Sir Dean and gave her a copy of the open issues they discussed: a hardware inventory, liberal pay scales with bonuses and profit sharing, rebates to the supporting countries, an economic impact study for each participating nation, a list of their satellites, and a discussion of their covert human assets around the globe. "We agreed to do that verbally and identify only functions, not names or countries," Bryan ended his report.

"That should be all right," Evelyn said. "We are making progress on our own internal review and I have a strong suspicion of one of our unit heads."

She thanked the team again and reemphasized the importance of their mission. "I will be passing copies of these reports on to the prime minister, your president, and the other members of the Security Council. Each has promised to send at least one person to monitor your work. Russia is also sending the former deputy head of the KGB, Piotar Petrovich. He may be helpful in your security review."

"Petey and I are long time combatants," Rid interjected. "He's good. He will be very helpful."

"Anything else?" Evelyn asked. She waited a moment and then said, "Let's eat."

The dinner was excellent and Rid even enjoyed the lamb chops. After the others had gone back to the castle, those staying at the manor house returned to the library.

"I must tell you, Evelyn, that we are getting outstanding cooperation from Sir Dean and his staff. Despite that, the three of us have a strong feeling that he has a hidden agenda. He is paranoid about eavesdropping on our conversations. Milt even found one of his troops with a directional microphone out on the moor tonight. We plan to ask him tomorrow to remove all bugs from this house, our cars, and our offices at the castle. In return, we will remove the three we planted in his office today."

"Did the tape reveal anything?" M was curious.

"No. He was not in his office most of the day and there is nothing incriminating on the tape."

"All right, Bryan, reach your truce," she said.

"We have another request," Milt put forth.

"And that is?" she queried.

"Bryan told you about the computer inventory and of our agreement to exempt his personal notebook computer. He says it only contains his own personal financial information, taxes, and his House of Lords schedule. Rid and I would like to have your permission to get a look at that computer to see if that's all that is there."

"How would you gain access to his computer? Doesn't he keep it with him?" M was being cautious.

"Both Rid and I have a great deal of experience with second story work. His quarters are on the third floor with windows in the castle wall. Our thought is to scale the wall sometime when we know he is out."

"If he takes it with him to London for his meetings, you would have a much easier chance. He maintains an apartment in Mayfair. Parliament is meeting this Thursday and Friday. The prime minister is to discuss his budget with them at a joint house dinner Thursday night."

"Perfect. It wouldn't take us very long to simply make a backup of everything he has on his disk. It's, no doubt, password protected but we can load it on our machine and break the code later."

"All right, gentlemen, you have my permission."

Rid said, "Thank you. You remember the treasure hunt we are working on for Jo? I am going to France tomorrow to get a team of U.S. Navy Seals started on a search of the Camargue. A former colleague of mine, Ken Merrill, was here the last two days. He considerably reduced the scope of the search from satellite photos. He left this afternoon, but sure gave us a leg up."

"Good luck with the hunt. It sounds like a nearly impossible task," she said.

"I'll be in London Thursday afternoon, Milt. Shall we meet at Dukes?"

"Yes, Rid. I'll scout out the apartment before you get there."

"Sounds like my team is all leaving me," Bryan groaned.

"You'll be getting Petey in return. You'll like him. He's smart like you, Bryan."

"Okay, I'll get him up to speed while you two are off to your nefarious schemes," Bryan quipped.

"Nefarious?" Milt bellowed. "Remember, we're the good guys."

"Let's all make sure it turns out that way," Evelyn said. "Now, I'm going to bed."

CHAPTER
34

The Camargue—Day 15

When Rid arrived at the private field outside of Arles on his F-16 fighter jet, there were two men in sharp navy uniforms waiting on the tarmac.

"Mr. Taylor, I am Commander Boudreaux Short of the Seals unit assigned to your mission. And this is my second in command, Lieutenant Vincent Liberto. We are at your service."

"Commander. Lieutenant." Rid acknowledged. "Boudreaux, you Cajun?"

"Yes sir. Born there in the bayou. This place you brought us looks a lot like home. Please, call me Buddy, that's my nickname."

"All right. And you're Vince?"

"Actually the team calls me V. A. for my initials."

"Okay, V. A."

"Our power boat is just over the bridge there. We can be at St. Maries in a little over an hour. The other six team members are there."

"All right, let's go."

It was noon when they arrived at the bottom of the delta. They had passed the town of Aigues Mortes on the way. As they traveled, Rid told them the story of Earl Ompree's lost crusade. He finished with, "I don't know how much they told you about the search. We'll be looking for Sir Ompree's treasure chest which has been lost since 1188."

Buddy said, "Sounds like a Cajun band without a fiddler—very improbable, but it will be good practice. You have any leads?"

Rid told him about the satellite photos and their estimates of size. "I brought this computer which has the photo CD-ROM disk. We started to cross off the improbables. I also will call our contact at the

Vatican to see if he turned up any drawings of chests used in those days. I'll call him this afternoon."

"The pictures will be a great help. We will organize our search using four two-man teams to check the most probable sites first."

They docked at St. Maries next to another similar craft where six more Seals were waiting. Buddy gave them a summary of what Rid had told him. They were excited. "A real treasure hunt. Pirate's gold. Is it finders keepers?" they asked.

"A real treasure, yes. Finders keepers, no. We've been hired by the family of the ill-fortuned earl to get back their property. Both the United States and Great Britain would like to see that happen as it would slow down the push for privatization of the military," Rid explained.

"That's a hot item. Everyone on our base in Norfolk is talking about whether we'll keep our assignments," V. A. said.

"It's really too soon to say. I can tell you we are doing a serious review of the proposal. This treasure hunt has become a part of that study."

"Let's hook up the computer and see what we got. H. Bunny, you do that," Buddy said to a tall blond Seal. "He's good at reading satellite photos."

"Anything else you can tell us?" V. A. asked.

"We know the box was made of iron, it was supposed to be waterproof, and it probably was thrown overboard during an attack by gypsies somewhere between here and Aigues Mortes. We tried to figure the size by estimating its weight. The loading of the old ships at that time probably wouldn't allow more than four men to carry it. If each man carried eighty pounds, that's three hundred twenty pounds. The chest probably weighed one hundred twenty pounds and that seems big enough to hold two hundred pounds of treasure. Particularly if some of it was gold bouillon."

"A chest that heavy would sink in the muck if it was tossed in the water," another team member said.

"That's what we figured. We're hoping that would help preserve the trunk intact," Rid replied.

"How did you figure all this out?" another asked.

"Our client has a letter written by the earl describing the loss of the chest and his failure to support King Richard in his crusade. Plus, we have seen the old ship's logs at a monastery near Salzburg. They've been stored in a salt mine all these centuries at constant temperature and humidity."

"How about that!" still another said. "Would that be Richard the Lionhearted?"

"That's right. The earl was to lead one of the king's armies."

"We'll have to call you Robin Hood, sir. It's a pleasure to be one of your merry men," a clean-shaven young man with a crew cut said. They all laughed.

"Finally, from what we know, we think the ship carrying the treasure was attacked before they could hide it. That's why we think it will be at the bottom of a channel between here and Aigues Mortes where they spent the winter."

Buddy said, "Most likely that channel won't be in the same place now. If the Rhone is anything like my Mississippi, the delta is a constantly shifting thing. Unless you control the water level with dikes or dams, that old river is just gonna keep looking for the easy way out."

"Will that make the search more difficult?" Rid wanted to know.

"Not if we go by the satellite locations. We have two smaller rafts that are airboats so they can skim the swamp to anywhere. We'll lock on to a location satellite which will tell us within four feet of when we're on a suspect site."

"That's incredible," Rid said. "Now, let me call my contact in Rome."

He dialed Monsignor Corso at the Vatican. When he came on the line, he said, "Good news, Rid, I've got it."

"Got what, Ricardo?"

"The picture. That is, a drawing of a typical chest used in the Third Crusade to carry each army's financing. It says it is fifteen cubits wide, eighteen cubits tall, and twenty cubits long."

"What's a cubit, Ricardo? I know you have researched that."

"You're right, Rid. I was just having a little fun. A cubit was the measure used in those days for selling cloth. Each cubit is one and nine tenths inches as near as we can tell."

"If our box is the same, that would make it about twenty-eight inches wide, thirty-three or thirty-four inches high, and thirty-eight inches long," Rid calculated.

"Twenty-eight point five, by thirty-four point two, by thirty-eight, to be exact."

"Did you hear anything from the abbey?"

"They called this morning, Rid, to say they found nothing."

"What you found should be enough. Thank you, Ricardo."

"Good hunting," the monsignor said as he hung up the phone.

Rid turned to the group and relayed the dimensions. "I feel good about our chances," he said to no one in particular. "Let's go upriver to Aigues Mortes where your government has booked us rooms at the Hotel Agricol. It's been there for several centuries, so perhaps the earl will come to us to show us the treasure."

"Dream what you want, Rid," said V. A. "I prefer to dream about my beautiful Maureen."

They arrived at the quay in Aigues Mortes, where the river ran inside the walls of the old city. They checked into their hotel. The Seals were assigned two to a small room. Rid had the only suite, so they were soon gathered there to begin mapping the search. Rid had ordered some bread, cheese, wine, and several bottles of the local beer.

"We like this assignment already. Let's hope we don't find that chest too soon," the shortest Seal they called Buckshot said.

"Just find it. If you can find it in less than thirty days, I'll personally sponsor a big weekend for you in London."

"You're on," they said as a chorus.

126

CHAPTER
35

The Camargue—Day 16

The next morning, all of the Seals were waiting for Rid when he came down to breakfast. They had already eaten after their five-kilometer run.

"H. Bunny has cut the list of possibilities down to about three hundred," Buddy began. "We have split them into four segments of seventy-five each for our two-man teams. Where there is less water the areas are larger, but we thought it best to divide them by number."

"That makes sense to me," Rid said. "Are you going to start this morning?"

"Yes. It will take about two hours to get all our equipment set up. We have to zero in on our location so the satellite system can work accurately. And we need a training review on the new handheld sonar. I'm the only one that has seen this new toy. It should work great in an application like this," Buddy bragged as he put a map in front of Rid.

The map showed the Camargue with red dots all over. Each dot had a longitude and latitude measure written beside the dot. The map was gerrymandered into four segments with the names Buddy, V. A., H. Bunny, and Buckshot written on the different pieces.

"We'll meet you at the boats at 10:00 if that's all right with you," Buddy said as he stood up. "You're welcome to ride along with me today if you want to see the process."

"That would be great!" Rid said enthusiastically. "I can work if you want."

"The toughest part is the digging. You can help with that."

Rid was at the dock at a 9:45. The boats were ready to go. They all started down the river together, but as they went south, the other three boats broke off to their assigned areas. Buddy went the furthest to the area between St. Maries de la Mer and Aigues Mortes, which they considered the most likely spot for success.

The day was both exciting and exhausting. The boats would work their way over a suspected site, dial up the satellite locator, then maneuver the boat to the exact location indicated by the latitude and longitude on the site. The two Seals would jump in the water and swim around and under the boat with their scuba gear and handheld sonar. When the sonar indicated they were zeroed in on an object that matched the shape and size of the satellite picture, they would take small spades and picks into the water and begin digging. This proved very difficult as the muck on the bottom was like trying to dig in ooze. As they practiced they decided they should use a long rod as a probe to find the depth of the object. If it was less than two feet, the Seal would force his hand down and hook the boat's winch to it. They would have the boat's winch simply pull it to the surface. The deeper items still required digging before reaching the winch depth.

They returned to Aigues Mortes at 5:00 P.M. Buddy's boat had raised five items: two truck tire rims, a traveler's trunk, a fish box off a commercial fisherman's boat, and a fish trap that was wood but had metal straps on the corners. They were pleased at the condition of the trunk. They pried it open. While it was not made to be watertight, the contents were identifiable as women's clothes, costume jewelry, and some rotten papers. There was a name and date etched into the metal. "Olga Pavrika, Budapest, 1764," it read.

The other boats had similar luck. They had each explored four sites.

"At this rate, if we're not lucky, it could take over two weeks to check all the sites," Buddy said.

"That's still good time. But, I have a feeling you guys will come through sooner than that," Rid said.

"You going with us again tomorrow? You can go in my boat," V. A. said.

"Not me," Rid replied. "That's too much work for a retired spy. Besides, I have to be in London tomorrow night for a little second story work. Something much more in my job description. Thanks anyway."

"How do you want us to stay in touch?" Buddy asked.

"Here's my cell phone and pager numbers. Call me each day when you finish. I can be back here in just a few hours if you need me."

"Sounds good."

"I don't want to over dramatize this operation; but, truly, the future of the world may be at stake."

"We'll find it, sir," Buckshot said.

CHAPTER
36

Buckshot O'Brien, one of the Navy Seals' team leaders, ran Ridley Taylor up to the Arles where he caught an early train to Marseilles. From there he took the noon British Air flight to London's Gatwick Airport. Having gained an hour by the change in time zone, he arrived at Gatwick at 12:55. He cleared customs through the diplomatic line and went downstairs to the rail terminal in the lowest level of the airport. From there, trains ran both to Brighton on the south coast and in to London's Victoria Station. The in-town connection ran every twenty minutes and the trip took just over thirty minutes. It was 2:05 when he emerged from the station. The sun was shining brightly, unusual for a spring day in England. Rid decided to walk the few blocks past Buckingham Palace to Dukes Hotel in St. James Place.

When he arrived, there was a message at the reception desk from Milt Young. It said, "I've gone to reconnoiter. Back by 4:00. Come to my room, 4714." Rid put his things in his room and then went to the dining room to get lunch. At 4:00 he went up to Milt's room.

Milt opened the door saying, "This should be a piece of cake."

"And hello to you, too," Rid replied.

"Oh yeah. Hi!"

"Tell me about the job, Milt."

"Sir Dean has a three-story flat on a quiet street in Mayfair. The alarm system is one with a code for keyless entry. Our decoder can handle that. Once in, all we have to do is find the computer and dump its hard drive on to ours. We can be in and out in ten minutes."

"Sounds good. When do we go?"

"Evelyn told me the Lords' dinner is set for 7:00 P.M. I'd say we go about 9:00 when the street will be empty."

"All right," Rid agreed.

"What about your search in the Camargue?"

"It is off to a great start. The Navy Seal team is really talented and the sophistication of their equipment is unbelievable. Using satellite location tools they can position themselves within a few feet of any object shown on our maps."

"Wow, the world is really changing. How long will the search take?"

"No more than three weeks. If they are lucky, it could be any day."

"Let's plan on being lucky. I want to see the look on Sir Dean's face when we tell him that his headquarters at Bodmin Castle belong to Jo."

"Me too," laughed Rid. "Let's prepare for this evening and then go to the bar for a drink. Dark clothes, I presume."

"You know the drill, Rid. I'll see you in the bar in thirty minutes."

After two Bombay Gins for Milt and two White & Makay Scotches for Rid, they went down the street to the Crown and Carriage Pub near the Mall. They looked like two Italian hit men in their black shirts and leather jackets. But then, in London, people are used to seeing all kinds of crazy dress. After dinner, they took the underground to Mayfair Station and walked to Sir Dean's. The lights were lit on the second floor.

"Oh oh!" Rid said. "Looks like Sir Dean has company."

"I watched him go in and out this afternoon, and he was alone," Milt replied.

"I'm going to climb that downspout pipe and get a look inside, Milt. You wait here."

Rid shinnied up the pipe and peered into a sitting room. The television was on and Franz Schwartz was sitting in a leather recliner watching a rerun of *The Benny Hill Show*. Rid slid quietly back down.

"It's Schwartz. What do we do now?"

"I checked. The alarm is turned off. Probably because he is there waiting for Sir Dean. Was that window open?"

"Yes, just a crack. It looks like you could get in," Rid answered.

"Good. You go ring the doorbell and keep Franz busy while I go in and copy the disk."

"Be careful."

"You too."

Milt climbed the pipe and was at the window when Rid rang the bell. As soon as he saw Schwartz go downstairs, Milt was in the room. A quick look told him the computer wasn't in this room. He went upstairs to the third floor bedrooms. As he went up the stairs, he could hear the voices below.

"Hello, Franz," Rid said as the door opened. "I'm looking for Sir Dean and was told he was here in London."

"He's out, Taylor. What do you want?"

"I wanted to see him privately, away from Bodmin Castle, to discuss the possibility of my joining the New Millennium team."

"You would turn on your friends?"

"If the money is right."

"I'm sure Sir Dean will want to meet you. I have to say I don't like you, but I do appreciate your expertise," Franz sneered.

"Could we sit down for a minute, and I'll write down my capabilities, my connections, and what I would want in return. Remember, I am in a position to deliver the United States to New Millennium."

"All right, come in to the reception room."

After fifteen minutes of writing, Rid figured Milt was done. He handed the papers to Schwartz, saying, "This must be kept strictly confidential for me to remain on the audit team. No one but you knows I'm here. If it gets out, I'm coming after you."

"I look forward to that encounter. I'll chew you up and spit you out for vulture food."

"We both know our time will come. For now, just see that Sir Dean gets my message."

When Rid left the house, he started down the street toward the tube station. Milt was waiting in the shadows at the corner.

"I got it," Milt said. "Thanks for the extra minutes. What cock-and-bull story did you tell him?"

"A real winner for such short notice. I told him if the price was right, I wanted to join New Millennium's team and spy on you."

"That's great. If they bite, we may want to go through with the ruse."

"Who said it was a ruse?" Rid smiled.

"Lady Joanna won't like you any more," Milt bantered.

"That's true. I better plan on just marrying her for her fortune after we find it."

"What makes you so certain she has marriage in mind?"

"I'm not sure. And there is another suitor, Reginald something. A peer of the realm from the Cotswolds."

"Ridley Taylor, giving up the adventurous life to settle down in Bodmin Moor. It doesn't seem to fit."

"You're probably right. Let's go see what we have on the disk."

CHAPTER
37

London—Day 17

When they returned to the hotel, Milt immediately set up his laptop computer and inserted Sir Dean's disk. When he tried to open the file, the computer screen read, "Access denied, password required."

"Here's our first hurdle, Rid. What would Sir Dean use as a password?"

"Try 'new millennium' or just 'millennium' or maybe 'King Dean,' or 'master.'"

"It could be a set of numbers too, like his birth date or wedding date."

"My brother uses his son's first name. But I haven't heard that Sir Dean has children," Rid canceled his own suggestion.

"Let's reason this out," Milt said. "I'll bet it is either New Millennium or the number one-one-two-zero-zero-one for 1 January 2001."

"Try the number first. That has to be the way he would want it."

Milt typed in the password and the computer responded with, "Welcome, Sir Dean. Please select the program you want to run from the list below."

The list read: House of Lords; New Millennium; Personal Investments; Quicken Financial; Speech Writer; Turbo Tax; and U.K. Online.com.

"Let's see what we get by clicking on New Millennium," Rid said looking over Milt's shoulder.

Milt moved the cursor to the New Millennium line and hit enter. A second menu filled the screen, reading Activities, Correspondence, Diary, Personnel Records, Personal Goals, Strategic Plan, Timetable, and World Leadership.

"His true plan could be under any of the last four. Let's try them," Milt said. He clicked on each in turn. The screen was the same for all the items on the menu. It read, "Access denied. Current security code required."

"This could take some time," Milt went on. "I may need help from one of our top code breakers. The stuff on the disk is probably all gibberish and the code turns it into English. I'll play with it tonight. If I can't crack it, we can take it back to Bodmin tomorrow."

"What about the deciphering room at Betchley Park?" Rid asked.

"Another state secret stolen by the Yanks. I'm still concerned about the mole at MI6. I'd rather control the disk myself."

"Okay," Rid agreed. "I want to call Sir Dean to see if he will meet with me tomorrow on my proposal. Then we can head back to Bodmin Moor."

"Sounds good to me. Now get out of here and let me concentrate."

"Let's meet for breakfast, Milt."

"Why don't I order it sent here to the room so we can talk?"

"Okay. I'll be here at 7:30," Rid said.

"Make it 8:30. I may be up all night trying to get the goods on Sir Dean."

"I hope you find it. Good night, Milt."

"Good night, Rid."

Milt looked again at the computer menu before him. "I wonder what 'World Leadership' contains. Is it a list of who is who now, or the way Sir Dean wants it to be?"

CHAPTER
38

Rid called Sir Dean's townhouse at eight before going to breakfast in Milt Young's room.

Franz answered, "Sir Dean Floyd's residence. Support world peace."

"This is Ridley Taylor, Franz. Is Sir Dean awake?"

"Yes. He is in his study preparing for today's debate in the House of Lords on the new budget."

"May I speak with him?"

"Just a moment. I'll see. I have briefed him on your offer."

After a lengthy pause, Sir Dean came on the line. "Mr. Taylor, how good of you to call. Mr. Schwartz has told me of your proposal."

"I'm due back in Bodmin Moor this afternoon. I thought if we could meet this morning it could be very beneficial to us both."

"I must admit that I am somewhat skeptical of your motives, but the opportunity is intriguing. The Lords start their meeting at 10:30. Can you come to my office at 9:30? I'll leave a visitor pass at the door."

"I'll be there."

After the call, Rid went up to Milt's room where a continental breakfast along with bangers and English breakfast tea was set on the desk.

"Morning Milt. I've just talked to Sir Dean. I am to meet him at his office at 9:30."

"Good. You are doing better with your ruse than I am breaking this code."

"Tough, huh?"

"Very tough. Each time you try a false code entry, not only does it deny access, it also changes the code for the next try. That means you can't do it through any normal process of elimination."

"With all that, there must be something incriminating in there," Rid stated.

"I would bet on that. I think we will have to take this back to Bodmin and let our cryptologists have a go at breaking the code."

"We also could ask Art Cragoe to have a look. He might be able to read the internal computer program."

"That's a good idea, Rid. We'll go back to Bodmin after your meeting with Sir Dean."

"He says his House of Lords meeting starts at 10:30, so I'll be ready before then."

"Okay. Come back here. I drove one of the rentals up, so we can leave whenever you get here."

"Let's eat before those bangers get cold."

Rid arrived at the visitor entrance to Parliament at 9:20. His badge was at the desk. He passed through the metal detectors without incident as he had left his pistol with Milt. When he arrived at Sir Dean's office, he found him in the outer office conferring with his staff.

"Just a moment, Mr. Taylor. I'm making assignments for today."

"That's fine. I'm a few minutes early."

"Everyone knows what they are to watch today?" Sir Dean asked.

"Yes, sir," they replied in turn.

"Now Ridley, may I call you Ridley, please come in."

"Call me, Rid. Everyone does."

"Rid it is. Tell me again about your suggestion that you go to work for me."

"I laid most of it out on paper last night. What I didn't put down was my motives. There are two besides the money. First, I feel certain that Milt Young's and my new venture, Janus International, will fail. It simply can't support the two of us. Milt is better than I am at solving security problems. My strength is in running covert operations. It would be a career challenge to help manage what will be the largest covert organization ever assembled. Second, I think I am falling in love with Lady Joanna Devon. By signing on with you, I will be close to her to continue our courtship."

"Both plausible motives, Rid. And as you say, they are in addition to the money. But what is my motivation to hire you?"

"I can provide you with a running update of the results of our audit and team meetings. I am the one who can deliver the United States as a yes vote on your proposal. Finally, I can tell you that Bryan Roberts is going to ask you for a moratorium on eavesdropping devices when you get back to your headquarters. We have found all your bugs both in our conference room, at Ruth's Place, and in the moor. We think you have found all ours. Without the bugs you need a new source of information. You need me."

"How do I know this simply isn't a scam for you to feed me false information?"

"You'll be able to tell if I'm accurate from your briefings with our leaders."

"All right, I will put you on our payroll on a trial basis. But before hiring you permanently, I want to see how the audit and vote of the Security Council turn out."

"That's fine. Don't send me any checks as that would blow my cover."

"I'll escrow your compensation at the level you suggested. We will pay it to you after a successful U.N. vote."

"That's fine. We have a deal."

"We have a deal. But I will be watching. You are to talk to no one at New Millennium but me. In my absence, you can talk to Franz Schwartz in an emergency."

Rid returned to Dukes Hotel where Milt had already checked them out, had the car packed, and was standing at the curb.

"Meet the newest employee of New Millennium, Milt."

"He bought it?"

"Wait till you hear what I told him."

As they drove out of the city, Rid went over his visit to Sir Dean's. "We have to be careful. He still doesn't trust me."

"Nor I him," Milt said as he pulled onto the motorway toward Devonshire.

CHAPTER
39

Bodmin Moor—Day 18

Rid and Milt arrived at Ruth's Place just after 4:00 P.M. They sent word to the team leaders to come to Joanna's house after dinner. Joanna had fixed only enough boiled beef for four. Bryan Roberts joined them at dinner.

"We got the computer disk, Bryan," Milt said, "but we can't read it because it's encrypted."

"That seems like he is trying to hide something," Bryan replied.

"I'd bet on it!" Milt continued. "Wait till you hear what your trained spy came up with to allow me to get in and out of Sir Dean's flat."

"You are looking at the newest covert operator for New Millennium," Rid said with a smile.

"What do you mean?"

"When we got to Sir Dean's place, it wasn't empty. Franz Schwartz was there in the second floor study. So I rang the bell to get Franz to come down while Milt went up the drainpipe and through a window. We knew I would have to keep Franz busy for at least ten minutes so I told him I wanted to go to work for New Millennium. I wrote out a long list of my capabilities. I also asked for a six figure base income with bonuses and stock options."

"Hell, I'd like to have that job," bellowed Bryan.

"In any event, I met Sir Dean this morning and I am now on his payroll. We ought to be able to use that to our advantage."

"We will. But we'll need to convince him your reports are accurate," Bryan suggested.

"Milt and I talked about that on the way down. Most of what I give him must be true. I need to give him advance notice on everything he'll hear in his meetings with the team leaders and you."

"Right."

"And you can help me convince him that my recommendation is key to the United States voting yes."

"Actually, it is. We need a storyline for the one thing we'll feed him that isn't completely true."

Milt broke in, "We could tell him about Jo's ancestor's royal decree."

"Why would we want to do that? It's our final trump card," Rid said.

"Hear me out. If he became convinced that he could lose his headquarters, he would begin to push very hard to get the vote over with. He would, no doubt, overplay his hand and antagonize several of the Security Council countries. Quite simply, he would show his true colors and that would squelch the deal."

"Perhaps," Rid said. "But we may be putting Jo in danger."

"I can handle it, Rid. Don't worry about me if we can stop him," said Jo, who had been quiet until then.

"It's not a bad idea," Bryan added. "Let's sleep on that one and see if we can come up with any others."

"The advantage of this idea is that it's true," Milt argued for his suggestion.

After dinner, the other team leaders arrived. Each one in turn reported on their recent progress. It seemed that everything had slowed somewhat as they were now into the details. Sir Dean's people were being fully cooperative. Bryan gave a report on Piotar Petrovich's skepticism that the plan was workable. He also reported on his interviews with key personnel of New Millennium. They all were happy to be a part of it and each had high regard for Sir Dean.

Then Milt told about his visit to London and acquiring the disk from Sir Dean's personal computer. Neither he nor Rid said anything about Rid working for New Millennium. Rid reported on the work of the Navy Seals in the Camargue. At the end of the meeting, they asked Art Cragoe to stay to discuss the computer disk. The others all piled into one of their two cars.

"Art, there appears to be a front end security program on this disk that changes with each use."

"There are such things, Milt. Given a little time, I should be able to get around it."

"That's what we thought. Here is the disk. Good luck!"

"I'll tell you tomorrow what I find."

"Good," Rid said.

"Better than good," added Bryan. "This could be the end of New Millennium, if the disk contains what we believe."

After Art left, Rid said, "I haven't even had my new job for a full day and you are already trying to put us out of business."

"Turncoat," Milt laughed.

"Easy come. Easy go. I'll be happy if we save the world."

CHAPTER
40

Bodmin Moor—Day 19

The next morning there was a dense fog over the moor and it was beginning to rain. Bryan, Rid, and Milt drove slowly to the castle through the mist. When they were close enough to see the outline of the buildings they had an eerie aura about them.

"There's some confirmation that Sir Dean has an evil plan. This place looks like something out of an old Dracula movie," Rid quipped.

"You're in England, Rid. We look like this most of the time," Milt replied. "What time is our meeting with Sir Dean, Bryan?"

"Not till 2:00 P.M. He's returning from London this morning."

"That will give us time to catch up on our work. Maybe we could sit in on some of your employee interviews," Rid said.

"Yes. After you sit through one with Petey or me, you'll each be able to do some yourself. Franz Schwartz came back from London yesterday, and he will bring us anyone we want."

When they arrived at their conference room in the castle, Art Cragoe was waiting for them. "No luck yet in breaking the code on Sir Dean's personal disk. It is, as you suspected, a security program on the front end that changes its password each time it is used."

"Can the code be broken?" Bryan asked.

"Of course," Art replied. "It will just take time. There are two other approaches that could be faster. One, there must be a separate book or list of passwords that tells Sir Dean the next one."

"That's not very secure," Rid stated.

"It doesn't have to be a separate list taped to his computer. It could be the first word on each page of a book or a poem or something like that."

"Remember how proud Sir Dean was about his library," Milt said.

"Yeah. Particularly about the biographies. Maybe one of them is the key," Bryan added.

"I'd vote for the biography of Alexander the Great," Rid quipped.

"Why is that?"asked Art.

"He was the first conqueror of all the known world at that time."

"He also seemed fond of Hitler's writings. Could be *Mein Kampf*," Bryan offered. "Let's send Jo to a bookstore in Exeter to buy some books for Art to try. Milt, make a list of as many of the biographies about world domination as you can. Art, you said there may be two faster ways. Tell us about the other."

"I can rewrite the security program or its internal table to follow some other method of assigning passwords. One that we will know."

"How long will that take?" Bryan asked.

"Two or three days. I'll start today," Art replied.

"Good. Keep us posted."

After Cragoe had left the room, Rid said, "That guy's amazing."

"Let's hope he is as good as we think," Milt added.

The rest of the morning they spent interviewing employees of New Millennium without any specific revelations. After lunch in the castle cafeteria, they prepared for their meeting with Sir Dean.

"What do we want to cover with Sir Dean today?" Bryan asked.

"The truce on eavesdropping devices," Milt answered.

"That will confirm to him that I can be valuable. I told him in London you would ask for that," Rid interjected.

"We also want him to describe his list of covert operatives," Milt suggested.

"Right, and I will give him a plain vanilla update on our activities while he was gone," Bryan added to his agenda.

"The big issue is the storyline I'm going to use to convince him I'm for real. Last night we talked about me telling him about our treasure hunt in the Camargue. I still don't like that idea as it may place Jo in danger. But, I can't come up with anything better," Rid lamented.

"We can protect her," Bryan affirmed.

At 2:00 P.M., the connecting door to Sir Dean's office opened, and he said, "Gentlemen, please come in."

Bryan gave a very positive report on the activities of the teams. Then he brought up the mutual need for trust. "We both have been guilty of trying to eavesdrop on the other. We removed two more bugs from our office this morning."

"And we still have one operating in here," Milt said as he rose and walked over to the bookcase to take the tiny microphone from the back of the biography of Lincoln. While he was there he took another glance at some of the other titles that might contain the security code.

"I agree. We must trust each other. I have been open with you as you have been with me. We have no need for spying on each other. There is one problem, however. Our employee barracks, recreation rooms, and cafeteria have built-in monitoring equipment. We review the tape recordings from these periodically to gauge employee morale."

"Perhaps for the short time we will be here, those tapes can be erased," Bryan suggested.

"It will be done. You can erase them yourself."

"Our employee interviews have been a tribute to your team building capabilities. They all speak highly of you and the leadership of New Millennium," Bryan said.

"That's good to hear. We do work hard at making them feel wanted, needed, and appreciated. Now, is there anything else?" Sir Dean rose as if to end the meeting. "Perhaps we can have tea together today."

Bryan picked up on that quickly and said, "I've scheduled a meeting with the communications team."

"And I'm set with the computer group," Milt set the stage for Rid.

"I'm available," Rid offered.

"That's great. I usually have tea sent in around 4:30."

"I'll be here."

The three returned to their conference room feeling they had scored a major victory. Milt added several conquerors to their list of code possibilities. Bryan said, "We got so excited with the fortuitous set up of a private meeting for Rid, we forgot to discuss his covert operatives list. We'll just put it on the list for our next meeting."

"Now help me finalize what I'm going to tell him about our treasure hunt," Rid changed the subject.

"I think you ought to tell him the truth," Milt said. "From the time Lady Joanna entered our office in Rome and how it lead us to Bodmin Castle in the first place."

"We need to be careful not to alarm him. He could send his security force after Jo!" Rid cautioned.

"I'll have the U.S. and British armies alerted. They can do a joint exercise on the moor," Bryan offered.

"I need to tell Jo what we are doing. She may want to go away for a few days. I also need to check on the progress of our Navy Seals," Rid said.

"Let's get at it," Bryan said as he left to meet with Dave Vanselow.

Rid called Jo on his cell phone and told her their plan. "Don't worry about me. I can take care of myself," she said to his entreaty to be careful.

"Not against Sir Dean's whole army, you can't. Isn't there somewhere you can go for a few days?"

"As a matter of fact, I do have an invitation to spend a long weekend in the Cotswolds. You remember my telling you about Reggie Byerly?"

"My competition. Yes! I think you should go."

"Reggie and I have talked about our ancestors and the crusades. It's possible that his ancestor, Sir Thomas Byerly was the one who took over the command of my ancestor's army. Maybe we could piece that together while I'm there."

"That would be good. But be careful of his romantic advances."

"I haven't seen anything but talk from you, so maybe I'll like what I find."

Rid then put in a call to Buddy Short's mobile phone to see how the Seals were doing. "Rid, my man, how you doing?"

"I'm back at Bodmin Moor and we've set the stage for me to tell Sir Dean what you're looking for."

"We got news. Earlier today, Buckshot's team pulled up an iron chest about the right size. It's completely rusted over and we haven't tried to open it. We're afraid if we use a blowtorch on it, the heat may disintegrate any paper inside."

"Good thinking, Buddy. I want you and anyone you need to help take the chest to Rome. I'll meet you there tomorrow evening. We can use the Vatican Museum's laser cutters to open the box."

He gave Buddy his office address in Rome. Then he called Jo again to see if she wanted to go to Rome.

"I've already accepted Reggie's invitation. I can't back out now. Besides, this is just one box. It may not be the one we are looking for."

"Probably won't be. I was just offering another trip out of here. You go on to Reggie's. I'll go to Rome alone."

"Poor boy," she said as she hung up the phone.

Rid's tea with Sir Dean was a winner. Sir Dean complimented him on the alert to the listening device moratorium. "I don't need those now that I have you."

"That's right, Sir Dean. And I have another story to tell." He went on with a vivid description of the search for Sir William Ompree's treasure. He started with Lady Joanna's hiring of Janus International, their visits to the Vatican Museum, the monastery at Berchtesgaden, the satellite photos, and the deployment of the Navy Seals. The only detail he left out was that a box had been found.

"I plan to go to Rome tomorrow to check our office. Then I will stop by the Camargue to check on the search."

"You haven't told me yet how this treasure hunt ties in to New Millennium."

"You are not going to like this. It is possible that the box contains a royal decree from Richard the Lionhearted granting Sir James and all his heirs this castle and all the lands between the moor and Launceston, debt free, forever."

"Impossible! It would kill our proposal. We couldn't move our headquarters and meet any proposed timetable. I would fight it in court."

"I'm an American, Sir Dean, but I always thought the king could do anything he wanted."

"Lady Joanna is the current heir. Are there any more?"

"Not that I am aware."

"What if she relinquished her claim? Say she sold it to me."

"That's a question for your lawyers."

"Perhaps it's a question I will put to Lady Joanna. I am very good at gaining cooperation."

"I've seen your dungeon, remember. But I wouldn't recommend doing anything unless the chest and decree are actually found. You might upset the vote by taking any unlawful action at this time."

"That's true. I like the way you think, Rid. But I also like to be prepared. I will draw up a contract to buy Joanna out of her manor house, including her relinquishment of any present or future rights to Bodmin Castle and its land. Maybe you would be able to sell that to her."

"I will try."

"Barring that being successful, I may have to take more direct action. To that end, I will discuss this situation with Franz. He'll know what to do."

"A frightening thought, Sir Dean."

CHAPTER
41

Rome—Day 20

Rid was at his office in Rome the next evening when Buddy Short and V. A. Liberto arrived.

"You found a chest? That's great!" Rid exclaimed.

"It looks like the picture you gave us," Buddy answered.

"And it's really heavy for its size," added V. A.

"Where is it? I want to see it," said Rid.

"It's in the trunk of our rental car at the moment. Not the best place," V. A. volunteered.

"Right. Let me call Monsignor Corso at the Vatican Museum. He usually works late and it would be secure there."

The monsignor answered his private line on the first ring. He was excited to hear about the chest and told Rid to bring it right over. When Rid, V. A., and Buddy got to the museum, one of the curator's assistants was waiting at the door. He found a small dolly cart to put the chest on and they took the elevator to the fifth floor.

"It sure looks like the real thing," Father Corso exclaimed. "Just think of it, a treasure chest from the Third Crusade."

"We're not sure it's the right one," Rid cautioned.

"Here is a copy of the picture I gave you of the chests used then. It matches the drawing," Corso countered.

"Yes it does, sir," Buddy agreed.

"Well," the curator said, "we will soon know. I asked my laser expert, Fred Stone, to come in to look at the chest. I see him coming to the office now."

Monsignor Corso introduced everyone. Fred Stone was a lay employee who had extensive experience in laser technology. He had done medical treatments and surgeries as a doctor in the United States.

His artistic interests lead him to start testing lasers on art restorations. When his work came to the attention of Monsignor Corso, he quickly agreed to come and work on the priceless treasures of the Vatican.

"First, let's try to get some of the rust off the lock and the hinges," he said. "Maybe we won't have to cut the top out."

"We were concerned about heat destroying any papers inside," Buddy said.

"That's the advantage of lasers. They are only hot at the precise point they touch. And we can confine that to less than a millimeter," Stone replied.

"Let's go!" urged Rid.

With that, Stone positioned the chest on a table that had a myriad of cross lines drawn on it. When he got the lock of the chest lined up, he switched on the laser. It began to flake off the rust in small layers.

"This will take some time," Stone said. "It will go faster if you don't all crowd around the table."

"Speaking of tables," Corso said, "I haven't eaten since breakfast. The three of you come with me to the dining room, and we can eat while Fred works."

"I could go for that," Buddy quipped.

"Me too!" said V. A.

"Sounds good to me," Rid said as the four of them moved toward the door.

The Vatican dining room was really a first-class restaurant with menus and table service. Corso suggested the tortellini in brodo as a first course followed by trout or veal picata. Rid and Ricardo had the trout. The two Seals, claiming they had their fill of being in the water with the fish, had the veal. The curator had also ordered a very good bottle of Frascati and a bottle of the Vatican's own red table wine from the pope's summer residence at Castel Gondolfo. After a tiramisu for dessert, the four eagerly returned to the lab.

"How was dinner?" Stone asked.

"Very good," Rid replied. "How are you doing?"

"The rust is coming off slowly, but I may have found something of interest. Look here above the lock where I've chipped it down to the base. It looks like there is a set of initials there."

They all crowded in to look. On a small brass plate attached to the chest were the initials "J. O."

"This is it," shouted Rid. "The crusader who lost his chest was the Earl James Ompree. You Seals are terrific. You've found it."

"This is exciting," the monsignor added.

"I won't stop the search till we see what's inside," Buddy said.

"How much longer to get it open, Fred?" Corso asked.

"At least four hours, Ricardo. I have to go slow so I don't cut too deep."

"I know it will be hard, Rid, but I suggest leaving Fred to his work, and let's meet here again at 10:00 tomorrow."

"I probably won't sleep at all, but I agree we should let your expert work in peace," Rid said. "Come on, fellas. I'll buy you an after dinner drink."

"I'm ready," said V. A. "This really is exciting stuff."

"Do we only get one drink? I'll need several if I'm to sleep tonight," Buddy added.

The three left the museum about 10:00 in the evening. They took a taxi to the Pantheon and sat at one of the outside tables in the Piazza della Rotondo.

"Do you think we'll find Richard the Lionhearted's royal decree, Rid?"

"We'll know tomorrow, boys. We'll know tomorrow," he repeated.

CHAPTER
42

Rome—Day 21

Taylor and the two Navy Seals were ushered into Monsignor Corso's office at 9:50. Fred Stone was there with the curator. The curator began, "We have both good news and bad. The chest is definitely that of Sir James and much of the treasure is intact. The royal decree, along with other paper items have turned to pulp. Apparently, the chest was not watertight for all the eight hundred years it's been in the muck."

"Too bad. I would have enjoyed seeing Sir Dean's face when we showed him the decree," Rid lamented. Then his eyes lit up and he said, "Anyway to make a counterfeit one?"

Corso replied, "It wouldn't stand up. We can't duplicate the paper and we don't have the Lionhearted's personal seal."

"I don't mean one that the English court would accept. I only want to use a fake to flush Sir Dean out into the open."

"That could be done. I'll have our best art restorer make one."

"What about the rest of the treasure?"

"The gold and jewels are fine. Plus there are a number of old coins that should be very valuable. Here is a complete list of what we found," Stone said as he handed the list to Rid. It listed: pure gold nuggets, weight three hundred pounds; assorted jewels, weight twenty-two pounds; fifteen hundred English coins, weight ninety-four pounds.

"That's a total weight of 416 pounds," Stone continued. "The gold should bring about $400 an ounce. The jewels will have to be appraised, but could be very valuable. The old coins should bring a tidy sum at a Christie's auction."

"Maybe Lady Joanna will get enough to buy the castle if the decree doesn't work," suggested Buddy.

"Yeah!" Rid commented. "If we can get the U.N. to vote no, he may be willing to sell. Ricardo, will you store the treasure until we can make arrangements to have it couriered to England. I'll find out where Jo wants it sent."

"Certainly. I have a small request of her as well. I wonder if she would consider donating the chest to the Vatican Museum's crusade collection."

"I'll ask her tomorrow. I'm going back to Bodmin Moor to give her the good news in person. When do you think you will have the fake decree, Ricardo?"

"Within a week. I'll call when it's ready."

"Buddy, you can stop the search. I'll set it up with Bryan Roberts to give your team liberty for the three days in London I promised you. All of your expenses will be paid," Rid said.

"The boys will enjoy that. You're a man of your word, Rid."

"I am. Except when I show Sir Dean the fake decree. Let's hope I can pull it off."

When he returned to the Janus office, there was a voice mail message from Sir Dean asking if the chest was found, and did it contain the decree?

Rid called him back to say the chest had been found, but it hadn't yet been opened. They were going to have to go slowly to remove all of the rust and other deposits, before opening the chest. It may still take a few days.

Sir Dean hung up the receiver and began to think of his options for dealing with a possible claim on the castle by Lady Joanna. "I don't believe she has any living relatives," he thought. "So if she were to die, who would push the claim?" he mused.

CHAPTER
43

Bodmin Moor—Day 22

Rid took the early morning Alitalia flight from Rome's Fiumincino Airport to London's Gatwick. There he connected with a commuter flight to Plymouth. He had called ahead and both Milt Young and Bryan Roberts were there to meet him at 10:15. Once in the car, Rid began, "The chest is genuine and full of gold, jewels, and old coins. Unfortunately, the paper has turned to mush, so there is no royal decree."

"That's too bad! There goes our ace in the hole," Bryan lamented.

"Not necessarily," Rid continued. "I asked Ricardo to have one of his experts make us a forgery."

"Good thinking, Rid. Can they do it?" Milt asked.

"He thought one of his art restorers could make one good enough to fool Sir Dean. But it wouldn't pass a carbon dating test or the eye of an expert from the British Museum archives. Hand me your phone, Bryan, and I'll call Corso to see if they have started."

He called the monsignor's private number. "Father Ricardo. Pronto," it was answered.

"Ricardo, it's Ridley. Good morning."

"Ah, Rid, I thought you might call. It goes well. After you left, I remembered we have an expert in recreating old documents here. He is visiting from Hebrew University in Jerusalem to make copies of some of our early Old Testaments. His name is James Marblestone, and he comes from Illinois."

"What does he say about my request?"

"He says he has the type of paper we need with him. All he needs to see is a copy of any royal decree issued by Richard the Lionhearted. We are looking for one now in our crusade files."

"We'll have someone look in London too. I'll get back to you," Rid said.

"Goodbye, my friend," Corso said.

"Ciao!" Rid answered.

Rid repeated the conversation for Bryan and Milt.

"I'll ask Jeremy Martin to get us a photo of a decree that we can fax to Marblestone this afternoon," Milt stated.

"We need to get the document as soon as possible. What I haven't told you yet is that Sir Dean called me last night to see if we had opened the chest. I told him it was going slowly and could take up to a week. He wants to be kept informed. And he is thinking about his options with Lady Jo. The longer we have to stall, the more danger she is in."

"She's not here," Bryan said, "and isn't due back from the Cotswolds until the day after tomorrow."

"I'll call her to explain what we're doing and see if she can stay there a few more days. She doesn't even know about the treasure yet," Rid explained.

"What's it worth?" Milt asked.

"I tried to do some figuring on the plane. There were three hundred pounds of pure gold. At sixteen ounces to the pound and $400 an ounce, that's $1,920,000. There are some four hundred different jewels and precious stones of varying value. While they probably weren't worth that much in the twelfth century, let's say they could average $6,000 each today. That's another $2,400,000. The most valuable will be the coins, according to Ricardo. He thinks coin collectors would bid eagerly for them at an auction. I may be high or low. I used $7,500 each. There are fifteen hundred coins, so that's another $11,250,000. That's almost $16,000,000."

"Wow! Lady Joanna is wealthy," Bryan said.

"Twenty percent of $15,000,000 is $3,000,000," Milt whooped. "A very good start for Janus's first case."

"Let's focus on solving the problem of Sir Dean and New Millennium, Milt. We can count our money after the case is closed and the world has been saved," Rid reprimanded.

"Right. But $3,000,000 sounds nice."

"It sure beats what I'm doing," Bryan commented. "How does one join your outfit?"

"For you, it would be easy," Rid replied. "If you ever want to leave the service, you just call us. When word of this find gets out, we'll have more clients than we can handle."

"Right on," echoed Milt. "We couldn't have found the chest without your help from the satellite photos and the Navy Seals."

"We should share our fee with you," Rid proposed knowing Roberts would probably refuse.

"Not while I'm in my country's service. You know that," Bryan answered.

"I fully expected that answer. It's the one I would give too," Rid said.

They continued to talk about the approach to Sir Dean, and decided Rid should give him a full briefing on the chest being found and the initials on the outside. He should reiterate it may take a few days for it to be opened by the experts at the Vatican and review the possibility of it containing a royal decree granting the castle to Lady Joanna."

"He's not going to like it. No telling what he might do," Rid said.

"That's exactly what we want to see. His reaction to the news may be what we need to sink his proposal," Bryan suggested.

"We have to protect Jo," Rid insisted.

"I'll call Evelyn and have her put some watchers on her. Where is she?" Milt asked.

"Somewhere in the Cotswolds at a Sir Reginald Byerly's home. I'll get her phone number from Henry and call her when we get to her place," Rid replied.

"We should be there in about twenty minutes," Milt said as they drove on toward Bodmin Moor.

CHAPTER
44

Bodmin Moor—Day 22

When they arrived at Ruth's Place, Rid went immediately to find Henry, the caretaker. Henry said Lady Jo left the phone number for Sir Reginald on her desk calendar. Rid retrieved the number and placed the call using his cell phone. The butler answered.

"Sir Reginald Byerly's residence. How may I help you?" he said.

"My name is Ridley Taylor. I'm a guest at Lady Joanna Devon's manor house and I need to talk to her. It is urgent."

"That will be difficult, Mr. Taylor. The lady and my master left about an hour ago on horseback. They took along a picnic lunch and I have no idea where they were planning to go."

Rid thought, *Uh oh. Things must be heating up.* He said, "I'm going to be gone this afternoon. Please tell her I will call again at 7:00 this evening."

"Yes sir. I will make a note."

Rid copied the phone number into his date book. He gave the other back to Henry to put back on Jo's desk calendar.

"I'll put it back on the calendar later, sir. After I've helped Margaret with dinner," Henry said.

Rid told the others that Jo was out of touch for the day, as they drove up to the castle. When they arrived, there was a note from Art Cragoe saying he wanted to meet with them. There was also a note from Sir Dean, asking Rid to see him.

"Let's get Cragoe down here first. I want to hear what he's found before I meet with Floyd," Rid suggested.

"They are probably all at lunch," Milt replied. "I'll go find Art and bring him here."

"Better than that," added Bryan, "let's go to lunch ourselves. That way, Rid can get word to Sir Dean that he'll come to his office, say around 2:00, and we can meet with Art right after we eat."

"Sounds good, I'm hungry," Milt said as he walked to the door.

They were correct that all the players were in the dining hall. They each greeted Sir Dean. Bryan and Milt said "Hello." Rid quietly proposed, "Two o'clock. Your office."

Sir Dean nodded. The three got their trays and sat down with the team leaders. They all continued to be amazed by the efficiency of the whole Millennium operation. They also each continued to have a sense that Sir Dean could have a hidden agenda. Art said he needed to meet with the three project leaders.

"Yes," Bryan replied. "We saw your note. Perhaps we can take a walk after lunch."

"That would be good," Rid said. "I'm scheduled to meet with Sir Dean at 2:00."

"Let's eat then," Milt said with a forkful of shepherd's pie on its way to his mouth.

After a quick lunch Art, Bryan, Milt, and Rid went outside the castle and started walking around the walls. Art began, "I have successfully written a new front-end security system for Sir Dean's personal computer. The information in his private files confirms all our suspicions. It is his plan to take over the world and to name himself the king of all."

"I knew it," Milt exclaimed.

"Tell us more about what you found," Bryan asked.

"Here are some pencil notes I made for this meeting with you. I also have printed out everything from his disk. I don't think anyone saw me but I've locked the printouts in my desk. I'll bring them to your place this evening. These notes give you a summary of each of his files."

As they walked, Bryan began to read, and then he would pass each page to Rid who, in turn, passed them to Milt. The sheets read:

House of Lords:
> *This is his schedule of meetings and pending topics for debate.*

New Millennium:

> *A copy of the overall strategic plan as given to you, but with parenthetical notes about his own true plan at each stage.*

Personal Investments:

> *Lists his assets. He has spent over £200,000,000 on this project and is near running out of money. That's why he is so eager to get it done.*

Quicken Financial:

> *This shows his cash flow and his current year tax status. They echo the problems shown above.*

Speech Writer:

> *Apparently he writes his own speeches. This file contains a record of every speech he has given. It also has as work in progress of his upcoming presentations to the Security Council and the General Assembly. Compelling stuff.*

Turbo Tax:

> *He has just started using this and has been trying to tie it into Quicken. Not much here.*

U.K. Online.com:

> *This is his connection to the Internet. He has a large mailing list database stored here of his supporters and operatives from across the globe.*

The pencil notes went on.

Within the New Millennium file are several sub files. The contents of these are:

Activities:

> *His calendar of meetings and events. Not much of interest.*

Correspondence:

> *He's very careful what he writes. This file contains copies of his letters.*

Diary:
> *A daily recording of the significant events of that day. Some of the notes are very revealing.*

Personnel Records:
> *Complete files on all New Millennium employees, including salaries and background checks. He has some very nasty people on his payroll, particularly Franz Schwartz.*

Personal Goals:
> *An explanation of why he feels he is qualified and ordained to rule the world. Will make great press for our side.*

Strategic Plan:
> *His true plan for world domination. It is the reverse of the other one. This time he shows the phony parts from the published plan in parentheses.*

Time Table:
> *He shows a commitment to seizing control by 1 January 2001. He notes that the new millennium actually begins then. He needs the U.S., Russia, Germany, England, and Israel to commit during 2000 to make it work.*

World Leadership:
> *The most damning of all. It lists the present leadership of each country and who he plans to replace them with from his own recruits. Example, a U.S. Senator will replace Clinton and Gore who are scheduled for assassination. He would overrule the constitutional passage to the Speaker of the House. This file also contains the names and positions of his covert operatives, including John Coale, M's deputy for internal affairs. Each had a monthly stipend and a Swiss bank account at the Gotleib Bank in Zurich.*

As each one in turn finished reading Art's notes, they voiced their excitement about what he found.

"I'm going to call M right away to tell her so she can brief the prime minister and arrest Coale," Milt said.

"And I'll call my director to have him brief President Clinton. They will, no doubt, want to have a press conference," Bryan added.

"When Sir Dean finds out we have him, all hell is going to break loose around here," Rid said.

"Remember, I asked for a joint U.S. and U.K. military exercise in the moor. I'll have them arrive tomorrow," Bryan answered.

"I'm on my way to meet with Sir Dean now. What, if anything, do I tell him?" Rid queried.

"Nothing. We need to have everything lined up before we spring the trap. Just stick to your story about finding the treasure chest."

"I need to check on that too, to see if Marblestone got the fax of a royal decree and how he's coming with the forgery."

"We don't really have to flush him out now, but the treasure ploy will buy us setup time," Bryan concluded.

They reentered the castle just before 2:00 and Taylor went straight to Sir Dean's office.

"Thank you for coming, Rid. Please sit down. What was the topic you all seemed so interested in during your after lunch walk with Cragoe?"

"You watched us?"

"Our surveillance cameras are on all the time. Remember, we let your people review and erase the tapes."

"Right. Art Cragoe was giving us a near final report on your systems. He continues to be very complimentary about their sophistication. Then he suggested we ask you one more time to let us look at your personal computer."

"We agreed that was off limits. It's personal financial records and my work in the House of Lords."

"I'll tell them. Don't worry about it. Let me tell you about my trip to Rome. The curator of the Vatican Museum believes my Navy Seals have actually found the treasure chest of Lady Joanna's ancestor, the Earl James Ompree who was the first owner of this castle."

"Damn. What makes them so sure?"

"Three things. First, Lady Joanna had a letter from the earl to his wife, written as he was dying in France. I have a photo here for you."

Rid paused while Sir Dean read the copy. It was easy to tell when he got to the part about Lionhearted's royal decree. His brow furrowed and he said, "Double damn! You said three things."

"Second, it was found buried in the muck of the Camargue in the general area it was lost. Third, the chest matches the type used during that time and we found the initials J. O. on the nameplate."

"This is indeed bad news. Have they been able to open the chest?"

"Not yet. They are using lasers to peel away the rust one layer at a time. They say it could take a week."

"Keep me posted at least twice a day on their progress. If that decree is found, I want to know it before any public release. Also, where is Lady Joanna? I want to talk to her."

"Her caretaker told me she was away for a few days, but he didn't know where. I'm trying to track her down to tell her we found the chest."

"Do not tell her that. I need time to sort this out."

"She knew why I was going to Rome. She knows we have a chest."

"Tell her what you told me. You found a chest. They are using lasers to peel away the rust, but they can't tell if it's the earl's or not."

"Okay, I'll tell her."

When Rid left the office, Franz Schwartz came out from behind a window drapery. "I still don't trust him, Sir Dean."

"Nor I. But his information is valuable. I want you to do several things. First, see if Tom Costa thinks he could break into the Vatican Museum and steal the chest. Find out where Lady Joanna is and kidnap her. Take her to my London flat and hold her there. Review our emergency escape plan and be ready to activate. Put our troops on red alert status in case we have to shoot our way out of here. I'm really concerned about whatever Art Cragoe was telling the audit leaders. Perhaps you could have a persuasive conversation with him in the dungeon. Just be ready to proceed when I say."

"I'll take care of all of it," Franz said as he clicked his heels and exited the office.

When Rid returned to the conference room, he told Bryan and Milt about his meeting with Sir Dean. He also scribbled a note that read,

"He wants me to locate Lady Joanna for him. And he wanted details of what Cragoe told us."

"Keep stalling," Bryan mouthed.

Rid nodded and said, "I've already had a long day having left Rome on the red eye this morning. I think I'll go back to the manor house."

"Take the car," Milt said. "The team leaders are to dine with us this evening. We can ride with them."

As Rid was driving back to Ruth's Place it began to rain. He thought, "I've really put myself in the middle between Joanna and Sir Dean. I have to protect her."

CHAPTER
45

Bodmin Moor—Day 22

As the clock in the front hall struck the first of seven bells, Rid dialed Sir Reginald's number. Again, the Butler answered, "Sir Reginald Byerly's home. How may I assist you?"

"This is Ridley Taylor. Lady Joanna should be expecting my call."

"Yes sir, I will tell her you are on the line."

Almost immediately, Jo came on the line. "Have you found it?" she asked eagerly.

"We have your ancestor's chest. It is full of gold, jewels, and rare coins. You're going to be wealthy."

"That's good news!" she exclaimed.

"Unfortunately, there is also bad news. All of the paper items in the chest were disintegrated. We don't have your claim on the castle."

"Too bad. I would have liked to be the one to stop Sir Dean and his evil enterprise."

"You still may. At my request, Monsignor Corso is having a replica made. One good enough to perhaps fool Sir Dean."

"Good. That may flush him out. How can I help, Rid?"

"By staying away from Bodmin Moor. He has already asked me to locate you and set up a meeting. I have told him about the possibility of the royal decree. He surmised you were the last living claimant to the land and his intentions for you are not friendly. I want you to stay away for a few days."

"Reggie has asked me to stay on here for as long as I like. Perhaps I'll accept his offer till you say it's safe."

"Reggie? Do I hear a touch of romance in your voice?" Rid asked jealously.

"He has been wonderful. Much more sophisticated and romantic than when we were together before. His father died and he has truly become the lord of the manor and has taken his seat in the House of Lords."

"Don't commit to anything until we can meet and talk," Ridley pleaded.

"I won't. But I want you to think seriously about changing your life from one of adventure to that of running a bed and breakfast."

"I'll do that."

"How is it going there at Ruth's Place?"

"Just fine. Henry is doing a good job and Margaret has been doing the cooking."

"Call me, Rid, when you have more news."

"I will, and you stay away from Reggie!"

"I can't do that. I'm his guest."

Rid hung up feeling a little lovesick, but reflecting on her request to think about changing lifestyles. He found he had considerable mixed feelings and began to think about how the finding of the chest and the exposing of Sir Dean excited him. "Maybe she is right, maybe she should marry a member of the peerage," he told himself. He was more confused than ever as Bryan, Milt, and the team leaders arrived.

"Where is Cragoe?" Rid asked.

"That's what we'd like to know," answered Bryan. "He came back this afternoon to bring us the printouts of Sir Dean's personal files which we have here. Then he went to his room to freshen up. When he didn't come to the cars with the rest of the team we got worried. Vanselow said he stopped by his room and it was empty. We went back to look for him with no result. Then we thought he might have come here early to talk to you."

"This is bad, Bryan. Sir Dean was most inquisitive about our walk with Art after lunch. He wanted to know what was on the pieces of paper we were reading. I told him it was a draft of the system team's final report and that it was positive. I don't think he believed me."

"He's probably being questioned by Franz Schwartz in the castle's dungeon," Milt said.

"He won't crack," Keith Wright interjected. "I've known Art for years. He'll keep whatever secrets we have."

Bryan raised his hand to quiet the buzzing conversation about Cragoe's disappearance. "It's time for all of you to know what we are planning to do. Rid and Milt were able to copy the files from Sir Dean's personal computer. It had a tough security clearance system on the front end that changed the code with each access. We asked Art to see if he could get around this and he did. We now have the printout of those private files, there on the table. They are very revealing as to Sir Dean's real intentions and will cause his plan to fail. With Art now in their clutches, we need to move quickly. I have a joint army of U.S. and British forces ready to start an exercise in the moor tomorrow at 8:00. Instead, we will have them surround the castle. Then we can go in to rescue Art. You all keep your teams in your barracks till after 8:00, then you can join us. We'll bring weapons. Jeremy, I want you to take these printouts to London now. Make copies for the prime minister and the president. See that they are sent to them before our exercise begins. I'm sure they will want to hold a news conference to announce the end of consideration of New Millennium's plan. What else, Rid?"

"I have Sir Dean convinced that I am working for him. I have told him that we found a chest of Lady Joanna's ancestor from the Third Crusade that conveys the castle to her."

"Have you such a thing?" Jeremy asked.

"No. But he has asked me to locate Jo, and I fear for her."

"We alerted the local police where she is. She'll be all right," Milt said.

"In any event, our audit work is done. You and your teams have done a truly outstanding job of serving your countries and the world," Bryan summed up. "Tomorrow will be a dangerous but exciting day. Now let's eat."

They called for Henry to bring them their dinner. But Henry and his wife were nowhere to be found.

CHAPTER
46

Bodmin Castle—Day 22

At the same time the team leaders were meeting at Ruth's Place, another meeting was going on in the castle. With Sir Dean were Franz Schwartz and his two deputy chiefs, Harry Bentsen and Tom Costa.

"There are a number of disturbing developments we need to discuss. We have learned that there is to be a joint military exercise in the moor starting tomorrow. Our informant, John Coale, says they may secretly be planning to take over the castle," Sir Dean began.

"If that's true, then they are on to us," replied Franz.

"We have to assume that. So we need to act fast. We have learned nothing from Art Cragoe. He has stood firm under all of the torture our dungeon has to offer. And now he is too weak to talk. Franz, assign someone to him in case he regains consciousness. On the other hand, we found a phone number in old Henry's pocket. It's the number of Sir Reginald Byerly's in the Cotswolds. Franz and I will take the helicopter there tonight to see if Lady Joanna is there. Supposedly they have found a treasure chest containing a royal decree granting this castle to her family. The Vatican Museum is working on opening the chest. Tom, you were in Rome. What can you add?"

"I saw them carry the chest on a dolly into the museum. If they are working on it there, it would be in their fifth floor workroom."

"Can you and Harry steal it?" Sir Dean asked.

"They have very good security, but with a little planning, I think we can."

"I'm sure we could do it," echoed Harry.

"Then you two charter a plane tonight and go get that chest," Sir Dean ordered. After they left the office, Sir Dean turned to Franz and said, "It looks like our plan is going to fail. I want all the money and investment papers out of the safe to take with us. I also want to stop in London to get our false passports and the cash that is there. After we eliminate Lady Joanna, we'll fly the chopper to France and go commercial from there to South America."

"What about Cragoe, Henry, and his wife?"

"We don't have time to deal with them. Just leave them in their cells." Sir Dean called his helicopter pilot and told him to get ready to fly. They cleaned out the safe, grabbed Sir Dean's personal computer, and went out to the pad where the chopper was already warming up.

When they arrived in London, they landed in a remote corner of Green Park within a block from Sir Dean's townhouse. They had gotten the things they were after and were back in the helicopter by the time a policeman had come to investigate their landing. Sir Dean grinned and gave a thumbs up signal to the bobby as they lifted off the ground.

"I've been to Byerly's place. It's just south of Buckland. Head for there," he told the pilot.

Back at Bodmin Moor, they had heard the helicopter take off. Rid said, "Do you suppose that's Sir Dean fleeing the coop?"

"Could be," resounded Bryan. "He has probably picked up on all the military communications about tomorrow's exercise."

"And, no doubt he's worried about our find of the treasure," Milt said.

"I'm really worried about Joanna. The local police are no match for Franz Schwartz," Rid stated.

"Why don't you two go to this Byerly fellow's place to see if they show up there. You can charter a plane at the small field in Launceton and be on your way within an hour. I can coordinate things here."

While Milt was arranging the charter, Rid called Lady Joanna again to find out where they should land and would someone meet them.

"Reggie and I will come to meet you," she said.

"Be careful. Sir Dean may be on his way there."

"We will."

CHAPTER
47

Buckland—Day 22

When Ridley and Milt arrived at the private airport just north of Buckland, Lady Joanna and Sir Reginald Byerly were there to meet them. Jo hugged them both, but she did not kiss Rid. "This is serious," Rid thought to himself. He found Byerly to not be what he expected. He was a tall, muscular, handsome man with a warm smile and a good sense of humor. As they were getting into his Rolls Royce to drive back to his estate, Byerly said, "We heard the sounds of a helicopter about ten minutes before you landed."

"Probably Sir Dean," Rid said.

"How did they find me?" Jo wanted to know.

"We think they kidnapped Henry and Margaret. They disappeared while we were having our meeting earlier this evening," Rid explained. "I know Henry had Sir Reginald's phone number in his pocket."

"I prefer Reggie, Rid. Do you think we are in danger?"

"Most certainly. That's why we're here. Sir Dean believes that Jo has a royal decree granting his castle headquarters to her. He made the comment to me that she was the last of her family still living."

"It also depends on who is with him. The helicopter probably only has seats for four, including the pilot," Milt added.

"I'd bet he only has his security chief, Franz Schwartz, with him. If his communications setup is as good as we think it is, then he knows about the army maneuvers at Bodmin tomorrow. He may be preparing to run. Having you out of the way, Jo, means the castle is still an asset of his to sell."

The car was approaching the front gate of Sir Reginald's estate. It was a large Victorian house with extensive gardens and lawns. There was a separate stable area in the back.

A seven-foot high brick wall surrounded the whole estate. They stopped the car outside the wall and walked silently to the gate.

"You two stay here," Milt said to Reggie and Jo. "Rid and I are trained for this type of work."

"I'm going with you," Reggie replied. "I put my hunting rifle in the boot of the car, just in case we encountered Sir Dean. And you need me as I know the layout of the house and grounds."

"Okay, but keep your head down," Rid cautioned.

"I'm not staying here alone," Jo exclaimed. "I want to see Sir Dean get his due."

"Not a good idea," Rid stated emphatically. "We would be watching out for you, rather than trying to surprise Sir Dean."

"I'll stay behind you among the trees. I want to see what happens," she implored.

"You are stubborn. Just be sure you stay out of sight," Rid capitulated.

Milt picked up his phone and asked Reggie for the local emergency number. He called the local police and explained the situation. They said their team assigned to watch Byerly's place was in the area, and they would have them come to the front gate.

"That's the answer," Rid started. "Jo, you wait here for the police and then lead them into the woods. Reggie, you could wait too."

"Not me. I'm a crack shot and I never did like Dean Floyd."

The three of them worked their way to the back of the house. Reggie had explained his security system. It had video surveillance on the front gate and front door.

The other entrances were simply alarmed, and he could disarm them.

"Do you think they may have seen us at the gate?" Milt queried.

"We have to assume so," Rid answered, "but we've been out of sight ever since."

"If they saw us though, they will be expecting three of us," Milt replied.

As they came around the back corner of the house, the floodlights came on bathing the lawn in bright lights. Sir Dean's helicopter was sitting in the stable yard with the pilot inside.

"No way to sneak in this way," Rid said.

"Let's back up. There is a cellar door in the shadows on the side. It is not alarmed as it is padlocked. I keep a key under one of the landscaping rocks." Reggie led them to an outside steel cellar door which was well hidden among the landscaping. He retrieved the key and the door creaked open.

"Shh!" Rid and Milt said together.

"Sorry, I should oil the hinges."

Once inside the dark basement, Rid said, "Here's the plan. Milt and I will lead the way. We will alternate or leapfrog each other as we enter new rooms or halls. You follow about fifteen seconds behind. If you hear shooting, stay put."

"And from this moment, no talking. No noise of any kind," Milt added. He then explained their hand signals for come, stay, left, and right.

They climbed the basement stairs that opened on the kitchen. They listened at the door. All was silent. Rid quietly opened the door and stepped into the room with his gun ready. No one was there. They worked their way down a back hall used by servants, listening at the doors as they went. When they got to the pantry door, they heard muffled sounds from inside and the door had been locked on the outside. The key was still in the lock. Sir Reginald opened the door to see his staff bound and gagged inside. He put his fingers to his lips to tell them to be quiet. They went on down the hall.

When they reached the security monitoring room, they could see lights under the door. Milt and Rid stood on opposite sides of the door. Then they threw the door open and jumped into the room with their guns raised. Sir Dean was sitting calmly at the desk watching the monitor.

"Well now, Mr. Taylor, it seems you have been playing both ends with me."

"That's right, and you're finished, so you better give it up now," Rid answered.

"I think not. Here, look at the front door monitor."

There, on the screen, was Franz Schwartz pushing Lady Joanna into the house with a gun.

Reggie had stayed in the hall. When he heard Jo had been captured, he slipped across the hall from the security room into a closet. In a few moments, he heard Jo and Schwartz enter the room across the hall.

"Here she is, Sir Dean. You two put your guns on the desk or she gets it right now," Franz said.

They complied.

"Now, where is the other one? There were three of you that entered the gate," Sir Dean asked. "Where is Byerly?"

"You're mistaken," Milt said. "There were just the two of us."

Sir Dean rose, picked up Rid's gun and hit Milt on the cheek. "I can count," he said. "Where is that cur, Byerly? He's been arguing against me in the House of Lords."

"Your proposal is dead, Sir Dean. We have copies of your personal files revealing your true intent. So, again, give it up. You're finished," Rid shouted.

"My time will come again. I can wait."

"The army will be at your headquarters in the morning. I'm telling you that it's over," Rid added.

"It's never over. I'm willing to disappear until a new opportunity arises," Sir Dean countered. "But, right now, I must finish with you. Sit down on the floor, all of you. Franz, you go find Byerly."

Franz started up the hall, away from Reggie's closet. Then he stopped, turned, and reasoned that if he was with the other two, the closet across from the security room would be the most logical place to hide. He returned to the door and began to silently turn the handle. The door burst open, throwing Franz against the far wall, causing him to drop his weapon. The hall was too narrow for Reggie's rifle to be effective, so he threw it to the floor and jumped on Franz. They engaged each other with their own talents. Schwartz was trained in all forms of hand-to-hand combat. Reggie was an amateur boxer. Both delivered a number of blows. They fell through the door into the security room and landed on the trio sitting on the floor. Rid started to grab for Franz.

Sir Dean raised his gun and said, "No, no."

While Sir Dean was watching the fight, Milt kicked out at the chair Sir Dean was in. It was on rollers and it spun around. Rid leaped to his feet and grabbed for Sir Dean's weapon. It went off, searing Rid's fingers that held the barrel. Rid winced in pain. Sir Dean spun around and started firing wildly. Milt took a bullet in the leg. The next, which was meant for Reggie, hit Franz Schwartz in the head. He dropped like a heavy stone to the floor, his eyes blank. He was dead. Sir Dean stared at Schwartz's death mask. That moment gave Rid another chance to go for the gun. This time he grabbed Sir Dean's wrist and twisted the gun free. It fell to the floor.

"You're finished for sure now, Sir Dean," screamed Rid.

"Not quite," Floyd answered, as he grabbed the other gun from the desk.

"What happened to the two local police who were with you out front, Lady Joanna?"

"Your murderer, Schwartz, shot them, you bastard!" retorted Jo.

"Good. Then it's time for us to leave. Take this cable we pulled from the computer and tie these three around their hands and ankles."

As Jo was tying her friends, Sir Dean began pouring oil from some of Sir Reggie's emergency oil lamps on the drapes and around the floor.

"Time for us to go," Sir Dean said as he backed out the door. "I'm taking Lady Joanna with me for insurance. I don't want some military plane shooting at my chopper." As he left, he tossed a match onto a drape and the whole room burst into flame. A moment later, Reggie's butler ran into the room. He had untied himself and he did the same for his master, Milt, and Rid. They grabbed the remaining guns and ran after Sir Dean.

"Take care of Milt. He's been shot," they screamed as they ran out the door.

The helicopter was beginning to shimmy when they reached the stable yard. Sir Dean was trying to pull Jo up into the seat. They began firing, away from her but at the chopper, with the bullets sparking as they glanced away. Sir Dean jumped further inside and dropped Lady Jo to the turf. They stopped firing as the craft roared away into the night.

"Damn," Sir Reginald said.

"Double damn," echoed Rid.

CHAPTER
48

Buckland—Day 22

After helping the servants and the local volunteer fire department put out the blaze, which did extensive damage to that wing of the mansion, Rid, Milt, Jo, and Reggie all flew back to Bodmin Moor in their charter plane. Milt's wound was clean, as the bullet had passed clear through the flesh of the thigh. When they arrived at Ruth's Place, they found Bryan Roberts meeting with the English and American generals. M was there also. Rid described the events at Sir Reginald's and explained that Sir Dean was probably on a low level flight out of the country.

"That's too bad," M said. "We will still charge him with treason, remove him from the peerage, and confiscate all his assets. We also have arrested John Coale and he has confessed to having the prime minister's receptionist in his employ. They are looking for her now."

"I sure would like to buy back my family's castle if it's to be sold," said Jo. "Even though I don't have King Richard's decree, Rid tells me I will have sufficient funds."

"I'm sure we can work it out, dear," M replied. "I'll talk to Tony Blair myself."

"Thank you!"

Bryan broke in with, "We had a call from your Monsignor Corso at the Vatican. He said two people, Sir Dean's men, tried to steal the treasure during the night, but the Swiss Guards captured them. They are willing to extradite them here for trial with the rest of New Millennium's leadership. Word has gone out to all the other countries to arrest their citizens who are involved. The U.N. Secretary General, Prime Minister Blair, and President Clinton will have a joint news teleconference at 8:00 A.M. New York time to announce the failure of the plan. We should have everything under control here by then."

"What about the military operation here?" Milt asked.

"We will surround the castle at 6:00. We will give the employees thirty minutes to surrender, and then we will enter the castle and take all Sir Dean's, excuse me, all Floyd's people into custody. The rest of us will go in right after the military says it's secure, to protect our team members and to find Art Cragoe, as well as Jo's caretaker and cook, Henry and Margaret."

"We should also alert Interpol and our network to be on the watch for Floyd," M added.

"We called them on the way down," Rid said. "If he planned his escape as well as he planned New Millennium, he will be difficult to find."

"He's probably headed to another country without extradition, where he already has an established identity," Milt guessed. "I suspect we're not finished completely with Dean Floyd."

"No, but his brainchild, New Millennium, is finished," Bryan countered. "Although, done right, it's not a bad idea."

"I agree," Evelyn added. "With the right governance and leadership, it's a good idea. Let's encourage the Security Council to see if they can't reshape the plan so that it would work for all. Just think of a century without any armed conflict and with added prosperity."

"We have a team of experts already assembled at the castle, Bryan," Rid suggested. "I bet within a week we could have a basic plan designed to leave with the Security Council for their future reference."

"That's a good idea," Milt chimed in, "but I've always felt the big problem will be getting the support of world leaders. They don't want to give up any of their power base. Floyd was going to take them by force. The U.N. can't do that."

Evelyn replied, "You're probably right, but I do want the team to stay and rework the plan before you disassemble. It will be a good blueprint for future U.N. discussions."

"Let's get to bed," Bryan said. "Early start tomorrow."

"All the rooms are full, Reggie. I have twin beds in my room," Rid said. "You can bunk with me." He winked at Lady Joanna, who scowled back.

"Okay, Rid, but I must tell you I snore."

"I'm so excited about the prospects of tomorrow, I probably won't sleep anyway."

"Good night, everybody," M said as she started up the stairs. "Big day tomorrow."

CHAPTER
49

Bodmin Moor—Day 23

The taking of the castle proved very easy. When the New Millennium security force saw the size of the surrounding army, and they realized their leaders had fled, they surrendered peacefully. The team members were all safe in their rooms. Bryan, Rid, and Milt went to the dungeon. They found Art Cragoe in bad shape, but alive. Henry and Margaret were unharmed in a second cell. When they were taken outside, they immediately went over to Joanna and Reggie to tell them how sorry they were to have been found with their phone number in his pocket.

"It all worked out, Henry. It's all right," Jo said to comfort him.

"Yes," echoed Sir Reginald, "it brought the whole thing to a head. And we almost caught Floyd."

"What about the mean one? That Schwartz fellow?" Henry asked.

"Shot and killed by Floyd himself during the scuffle," Jo replied. "Floyd tried to take me hostage, but Sir Reggie saved me. He was wonderful."

"I had help, dear."

"Yes, but it was you that came to all of our rescues," she said as she kissed him

Ridley observed the embrace from the castle entrance and knew he had lost Jo to the English lord. As he approached them, he said, "If you two lovebirds will break apart for a minute, I have a suggestion. After we wrap up here, I suggest we all go to Rome to inspect your ancestor's treasure."

"Yes, let's go," chirped Jo excitedly.

Bryan said he would arrange for a military transport flight for them. They could use it to transport the treasure to Lady Jo's bank in

London. He would arrange for an armed military escort. Jo, Reggie, Rid, and Milt were on their way to Rome before noon.

They called Monsignor Corso to tell him they would be at the museum by 5:00 P.M. When they arrived, the sight of the treasure awed them all. It looked like something out of an old pirate movie. Monsignor Corso and his staff had carefully cleaned and catalogued each piece. "Our best guess," he said, "is that the value is somewhere between twenty and twenty five million British pounds. About thirty-two to forty million dollars. It could be more at auction."

"Wow!" exclaimed Joanna.

"The real unknown is the old coins. If they were put in individual cases with a certificate of authenticity, collectors would pay handsomely for them. I would love to have one for our museum."

"Take your pick, Father. You have earned it."

"Thank you, my dear. We will display it proudly with our other artifacts of the Third Crusade. Did Rid tell you we would also like to display Sir James's chest. It could be on loan to the museum from your family."

"You may have it as a donation from my family."

"While you're in a giving mood, Jo, Rid and I would like a coin too. We also have the one Ricardo gave us of Janus from our Faust affair. We could start a collection," Milt stated.

"I owe you two a lot. When I came to you with this problem, you immediately went to work. I was always sure you would find the treasure. You may have the coins. And your share will be twenty percent, as agreed."

"That will keep Janus in business for quite a while," Rid said. "Maybe you two would like to join our advisory board. The current group includes Countess Liesel von Anton of Corfu, Clark and Lyn Keene from Cape Elizabeth, Maine, and Monsignor Corso. They were all involved in the Faust affair. You would be great references for us and it would give you an excuse to come to Rome twice a year."

"We would like to be involved. Saving the world is an exhilarating experience."

"We also have for you the forgery of King Richard the Lionhearted's royal decree granting Bodmin Castle to Sir James. Jim

Marblestone did a masterful job. It's not worth anything but it will be a memento of this long lost, but now found, treasure."

"Splendid. Reggie and I will hang it along with our two families' coats of arms over the main hall's mantle," Jo said as she was looking over the jewels. "May I see this?" she said as she picked up a three-carat diamond.

"It's yours," Ricardo answered.

"It's gorgeous!" she said with glee. "It will be for my wedding ring. Reggie and I have decided to get married. Once we have the castle with its new dormitories, we plan to open a finishing school for young ladies."

"Sounds less exciting than saving the world," Rid said, "but I want to wish you both the best of everything. Our twenty percent of the diamond will be our wedding gift to you."

Jo gave Milt and Rid a big hug, whispering in his ear, "We both know you'll be happier doing what you're doing now."

"You've got a hell of a guy in Reggie. I like him."

"Thanks Rid," she said as they pulled apart.

EPILOGUE

Christies did a fantastic job of auctioning the treasure. They had the coins set in little replicas of the treasure chest with a pull out drawer for the certificate of authenticity. When the items were all sold, the net after the auction fees was just shy of £27 million sterling. That's $43 million dollars. Janus's fee was rounded to $8.6 million, leaving Lady Joanna with $33.4 million or almost £21 million.

She and Reggie bought the castle from the government for £4 million. They moved in and everyone attended the wedding ceremony in the main hall where the royal decree hung over the fireplace.

The conversion of the barracks and offices into dormitories and classrooms was in full swing. They planned to be ready for their first class of young ladies in the fall of 2001. They decided to name it Sir James School in honor of Jo's ancestor who provided the funding eight hundred years earlier.

In her toast at the reception, Jo proudly said, "This school will now fulfill some of the concepts put forth by the castle's previous owner. It will prepare young, talented women for their own 'New Millennium.'"